I, MOMOLU

I, MOMOLU

BY LORENZ GRAHAM

Illustrated by John Biggers

Thomas Y. Crowell Company
New York

56597

BY THE AUTHOR

~~~~~~~~~~~~~~~~~~~~

South Town
North Town
How God Fix Jonah
Tales of Momolu
I, Momolu

To Jonathan, David, and Rebecca
Hoping that their bright eyes will look upon
the wonders of many lands

I, MOMOLU

1

It was a good day's work, and Momolu was tired. At the side of Flumbo, his father, he was harvesting rice. He liked to hear the soft swish of many knives, the gentle sound of the falling bundles, the talk and the laughter of those who worked.

Flumbo stopped and straightened himself. From his belt he took a cloth and wiped his body. Momolu slowed his pace but kept cutting, looking sideways at his father. Flumbo, like all those who worked, wore only a loincloth. The rolling muscles moved smoothly under his glistening skin. Strong he was—strong and good and wise.

Flumbo smiled. "It can be my son is tired," he said. "A boy can do the work of a man but not for too long."

"My body is not too tired," Momolu said. He ran his thumb along the edge of his blade. "My body is not too tired, but my knife no longer cuts well."

Flumbo nodded. "True," he said. "Under the tree is my sharpening stone. You must get your knife ready for tomorrow."

As Momolu turned away, he called to his friend Dairku. "I go to sharpen my knife."

Dairku straightened up, laughing. "I know. You go to rest your back," he said.

Dairku, like Momolu, was fourteen years old. His father, Logomo, was chief of the town of Lojay. One of the smallest towns in the Liberian interior, Lojay lay far from the coast and far from the roads and lines of frequent travel.

Dairku had come to work in Flumbo's field with his uncle, Nisa-Way. They had started cutting early that morning when the members of what Flumbo called his five-man club had arrived to help. In the morning Momolu had worked with the rising sun at his back. When it stood overhead, the women had brought food—great bowls of rice with palm oil and cups of soup seasoned with fish.

The cutters worked in an uneven line moving

westward. The sun had long since passed over-head, and was moving down now toward the low hill that lay between Flumbo's land and the town. Nearly half the rice had been cut. Ahead of them it stood waist-high, straw-yellow now in its ripe-ness, bending in waves with the afternoon breeze. Behind them the stubble stood ragged, half as high as the knee. It would take all of another day, perhaps more, to finish harvesting Flumbo's rice. Then the members of the club would move on to work one day or two or three in another member's field.

Momolu would not have left the field to rest while the others worked, but he was glad for an excuse to sit cross-legged on the ground in the shade of the mango tree's low branches. He rubbed the knife hard along the biting edge of the stone. It was a good knife, the blade half again as long as Momolu's hand. Flumbo had brought it home from the trading station, and he had shaped the handle with leather thongs to fit Momolu's fingers. As the blade crossed the stone it seemed to sing, and for just a little time after it came away from the stone, the note hung in the air.

Momolu was listening and enjoying the singing

of the steel at the end of each stroke when he knew there was another sound in his ear. He stopped to listen. His head went first to one side and then to the other and then turned back again to catch the sound. For a while he heard nothing. Then it came—a steady, even, one-two beat. It was the sound of a drum, but not of such a drum as Bama, Lojay's chief musician, or anyone else in town would be beating. For a moment Momolu was sure he heard it. Then it was gone again.

In the field they were still working steadily. No one else had heard the drum. He would have to tell them about it although it might well be that his friend Dairku would only laugh and tell him that he had slept in the shade and dreamed. Momolu was sure it was not a dream drum, and he thought from its beat that it was bringing trouble.

Out in the field Flumbo straightened himself and shouted to his friends. "Time for work is finished now. Soon the sun will go for sleep. Every man must turn from work and find his food and rest. Come we go."

There were some who said it was too early to stop, at which Nisa-Way said with a laugh that he himself had only started, that all might go and

leave him, and he would finish the field by himself. When they came again in the morning, the rice would be cut and carried to the town and threshed and put into bags. The harvest would be over.

"I heard a drum," Momolu called as he moved across the field toward the others. "It was not a drum from Lojay. Travelers."

"What?" Nisa-Way made a great show of surprise. "Momolu heard a drum! Another drum! Today many people are traveling."

"But there was something else." Momolu wished he could explain.

Some laughed, but Flumbo said, "The boy has a good ear for drums. Many times he catches their sound and knows the meaning long before any other one."

It was true that Momolu was often among the first to learn what was being told on the drum. When there was trouble or joy or news of travel or calls to celebration, the news was passed from village to village by the beating of drums.

"If there is news, Bama will know," Nisa-Way said, and all agreed as they set about to make for each man a great bundle to carry on his head.

Nisa-Way, who had said he would work all night, was the first to be ready to leave, and he had the largest bundle. Flumbo was the last. He helped the others get started, taking time to balance the awkward loads on the heads of Momolu and Dairku. Although Flumbo was very strong and could work as well as any other, he walked with a limp. Years ago his left leg had been torn by an alligator. The wounds had healed, but the leg was stiff.

Momolu said nothing more about the drum. He did not hear the sound again, and with all the talking, no one stopped to listen. As they moved along the trail that wound through the heavy growth of forest on the hill, he could hear nothing but the dry rustle of the bundle on his head. It was hot, and he had to keep his eyes on the ground to watch the way because the stalks drooped down over his eyes and around his head nearly to shoulder level.

From all the fields around the town, the men were bringing their unthreshed rice and piling it by their homes in great stacks. Flumbo's house was one of the largest in Lojay, and his stack was almost as high as the peak of its palm-leaf roof.

When Momolu had placed his bundle on the pile and shaken himself free from his burden, he looked around. The stacks made the town look crowded, as though new houses had suddenly sprung up. Children were playing in the softness of the grassy piles. Women were preparing the evening meal, moving carefully about their fires, guarding against a stray spark, which might set the rice straw ablaze. Few men were in sight, and soon after they arrived, Flumbo and his friends started toward the palaver house in the half-moon center of the town. Momolu and Dairku ran ahead of the men.

The palaver house was the town's meeting place. It was egg-shaped with a high roof supported by carved posts, and its front wall was only waist-high so that those standing outside could see and hear as well as those seated on the hard clay floor inside.

But no one was inside now. All were standing outside, watching Bama, the town's best musician and the maker of the finest drums in all the land.

Bama was seated astride the ridge of the thatched palm-leaf roof. One of his assistants was with him. The other man was holding a long log

drum, and Bama was listening with his ear pressed
to one end of it.

"What is the news?" Dairku asked as he and
Momolu saw a friend of theirs in the throng.
"What is the news, Billidee?"

"A drum!" Billidee answered. "We have heard
a strange drum. It is not the sound of a drum of
the Kewpessie people. Your father, Chief Logomo, says it can bring trouble. Bama listens to
see which way it comes and whether the people
move toward Lojay or only pass through the countryside."

"It is the drum I heard at the farm," Momolu
said.

"True," Dairku agreed. "Look how Bama's
drum is pointing. It is from upcountry that they
come."

Bama straightened up, turning away from the
long log drum. "It is the drum of marching soldiers," he announced to those below on the
ground. "The trail they make will bring them to
Lojay."

As Chief Logomo's own personal drummer
rapped out the call of assembly on his small underarm drum, the chief and the old men of the

council filed into the palaver house to take their places on the raised platform at one end.

Standing close beside the great chair on which Chief Logomo sat was Bomo-Koko, the high priest. He stood a full head higher than any of the others, straight and silent as though he were only a decorated post. A carved wooden mask covered his head. A robe of black monkey fur hung from his shoulders to the ground. The people knew that inside the costume was a man, but they always thought of Bomo-Koko, their prophet and worker of magic, as the strange thing they saw.

Logomo did not wait for a member of the council to speak for him.

"My people," he said, and every other voice was stilled. "We have heard the drumbeat of soldiers. It may be that they come to bring us friendly greeting. If that be so, we shall make them welcome. It may be, they come to bring us trouble. If that be so, we must find a way to have them leave us in peace. How they come, we cannot change. How they leave—that is our part to say."

He stopped and looked about him. Inside and outside, the people agreed with his words, and many of them said, "It is so."

"Now hear my words," Chief Logomo went on. "Let every man make his heart lie down while the soldiers are in Lojay. Let us fill their bellies with rice and meat and palm oil. The guns of the soldiers are many, and the power of government is strong past ours."

Logomo told all the people then just what they were to do. Food was to be prepared for all the strangers. The town guesthouse was to be cleaned for the soldiers' leader. Those who could move in with neighbors should do so and leave their homes free for the soldiers.

The palaver did not last long. Everybody hurried off to make preparations. Momolu ran to the river to wash before putting on his good robe. Back at his house he ate his palm butter and rice rapidly, without sitting down.

The sun went down. Those like Flumbo who owned lanterns lit them, others lit palm-oil lamps. The men of Lojay did not say much, but the women were talking excitedly about the extra food they were starting to prepare. Great kettles of rice were being boiled at every house. Cassava and eddoes and yams were put into the fire to roast. Smaller soup pots bubbling with chicken and fish and every kind of meat stood like little brothers beside the big rice kettles.

It had been planned that the people would not gather until they were called. Every man was to stay at his own home. Momolu generally wanted to follow the men's example, but tonight he slipped away and joined Dairku and Billidee and some of the older boys at the place where the trail led over the first hill beyond the edge of the town.

The half-moon was very bright; its light seemed to fill the valley. It showed all the boys dressed in their best. Momolu at fourteen had grown so much in the past year that he was almost the size of a man. His robe was beautifully made of blue-and-white striped cloth with a star design on the front and another larger star on the back, but it was too short for him; it reached scarcely to his knees. He comforted himself with the thought that it was not so short as Dairku's robe, and Dairku was the son of Lojay's chief.

"When I am a man," Billidee said, "I will be a soldier and journey to all the far places."

"And you will fight?" Momolu asked. "And kill people?"

Billidee was fat and good-natured. He did not

like to fight, and he was so seldom angry that one could not think of him killing anything.

"If I had to fight, I would fight," he said, jumping first on one foot and then the other. "And if one came to kill me, I would kill him first. So it would be."

As they listened and waited for the strangers to come, they could tell from the sound when the drum came over the far hill. Now from the town they could hear another drum coming.

It was Bama who came, led by two men carrying torches. Bama played his underarm drum and danced his welcome to the visitors. His high leopard-skin hat swung from side to side, the fringe of long, black monkey fur waving with the movement of his head. His robe was yellow and shone like gold. With each step the bells on his yellow goatskin slippers made little jangling sounds. His drumbeat was quick; the pitch so high, it was like a woman singing.

From the forest above on the hillside came a call. When Bama was a few steps away from the heavy growth of bush, two men dressed in the clothes of soldiers came down the trail. They marched very straight, one behind the other. Next came the log drum borne on the stooped shoulders of a man wearing only a loincloth. Behind came the soldier drummer. With two sticks, curved at the head into knobs, he struck the drum, and with each blow, sent out a crashing sound.

Immediately after came four men bearing the leader in a hammock. The hammock swung from a covered wooden frame which rested on the heads of the carriers. Then came a line of soldiers—Momolu counted twenty—all dressed the same way in brown khaki with short-sleeved shirts and knee-length breeches, their legs bound in khaki cloth from ankle to knee. Each head was topped with a small red cap with a black tassel swinging from side to side. Every soldier had his gun, held in place on his right shoulder. In the wavering light of the torches they looked as if they might have all been brothers, and as they marched they moved as one, for all stepped with the right foot together, then all stepped with the left foot together. It gave Momolu a funny feeling in his stomach to see them marching so. Behind the line of soldiers came carriers with boxes and heavy bundles on their heads.

Bama with his drum and his torchbearers had

turned to lead the procession down into the town of Lojay. Around the house of Chief Logomo and on to the palaver house, they marched. There the first soldier called out an order, and all the others knew just what to do. They moved together forming a straight line, their khaki-wrapped legs pumping up and down. Then at the call, all turning so that they faced the chief, they stood with their feet beating time until the next shouted order, when they stopped all at one time and brought their guns down from their shoulders to stand erect and wait.

There were many torches held high, and throughout the town the women had put fresh wood on the fires to make the town bright. All were quiet while Chief Logomo and the leader of the soldiers stood and spoke together.

Momolu edged himself as close as he dared. He could hear the talking, but he could not understand the words.

Dairku spoke softly beside him. "They talk the American way," he said. "My father can talk the American way because he has traveled. It is the speech of government."

The leader of the soldiers was smiling. His

clothing was not like that of the others. The sleeves of his shirt and the legs of his pants were long. On his head there was no round cap but a large hat, a helmet such as traders wore. He was smiling as he talked, and Logomo's face answered the smile, but the old men of the council who stood behind their chief did not echo the smile. Looking very serious, they watched and waited to learn what business brought the visitors.

While the leader turned and spoke to the soldier who had shouted the orders at the men, Logomo turned to his councilors behind him. "The captain of the soldiers brings friendship's greeting from the great government of Liberia," he said. "He comes in peace. The people of Lojay welcome him and his warriors in peace."

At this the men of the council smiled, and every man set about his task. Bama made his drum ring out. The soldier shouted to his men. Men of the council called to those who stood about.

In the shelter of the palaver house, the soldiers made a row of all their rifles and neat piles of all their boxes of goods. Then they were led by the men of Lojay to the houses where they were to eat and spend the night.

2

Momolu turned to Dairku beside him. "I am sure," he said, "that my father will bring a soldier to our house. Come, we will talk with him."

"Not so," Dairku replied. "None of these soldiers belong to our tribe. They will not be able to speak our tongue."

"But they travel. So they must be able to speak with all the tribes," Momolu insisted.

"True, they travel," Dairku said, "but only their leaders have to speak to the people, and then they use the American tongue and talk only to chiefs and wise men who know the speech of government. You will see."

The people of Lojay were of the Kewpessie tribe. There were many towns of Kewpessie people in that part of Liberia. The chief of each town was a member of the tribe's council under the leadership of a paramount chief. It was said of the Kewpessie people that they had always wanted only to live in peace. Set apart from others by rows of mountains, their own land was hilly with scarcely enough level valleys for their small farms. There were no plantations of rubber or coffee. There were no roads or bridges for motor-cars, so Momolu and most of the people of Lojay knew little about the outside world.

Most of the houses had but one room. Round in shape, with walls of clay and cone-shaped roofs of layer on layer of palm leaves, all of them faced toward the Tamby-Oway River. The rows of houses curved uphill around the open section where the palaver house stood.

Only the important people in Lojay had more than one room. Chief Logomo had a house of eight rooms, built in a square with all the rooms opening toward an inner court. At the close of the palaver he started walking toward his home at the upper end of the town. The captain walked beside him. The old men of the council followed, two by two, in a line behind them.

Bama led the way, beating his drum and moving lightly from side to side in dancing steps, and as he beat his drum he sang a song describing the handsome looks, the great strength, and the brilliant courage of Lojay's guest, the captain, the mightiest soldier in the land.

Dairku took Momolu's arm. "Come to my house," he said. "My father will try to please the captain with good things to eat, with palm wine, and with music and dancing. Many people will be there."

"At my own house my father will have a guest," Momolu said, "and there will not be so many other people. I myself will have the chance to talk with our guest."

"He will not talk to you." Dairku was very sure. "He would not talk to you if he could. You will see."

Momolu started for home, fearing that Dairku was right, hoping that he was mistaken.

Flumbo, the father of Momolu, said of himself that he was not an important man, but Momolu knew that all the people looked at him with respect and admired his three-roomed square house. Besides the three rooms it had a porch sheltered from the sun and rain by the pyramiding roof. Portee, Momolu's mother, was proud of her porch and liked to have her friends, whom she called sisters, visit with her in its shelter.

When Momolu arrived home, he saw that there was indeed a visitor. Flumbo had been given the honor of housing as his guest none other than the soldier who shouted orders. The soldier would be able to have a room to himself, and Flumbo's family would still not have to stay with friends and give up the house.

The soldier was not a Kewpessie man, so his speech was not known to the people of Lojay. Bowing and smiling, he took his place on a low stool, and Portee placed on the ground in front of him the kettle of rice, the pot of soup, a jar of water, and a decorated gourd bowl which had never been used.

Before he started to eat, the soldier poured water into the bowl, and with the knife from his belt, stirred into the water a few grains of rice and a little of the soup. He rose then and moved away from the fire. With his back to those who watched him, he lifted his head and spoke a few words in his own speech, then emptied the bowl on the ground. Momolu knew it was a libation, a sacrifice to the god the soldier worshiped or to the devil he feared

As he ate, the soldier smiled and with sounds and gestures, made Portee know that the food was good. When he could eat no more, he unwound the wide blue sash from his waist and patted his full stomach.

With signs and using his own Kewpessie words, Momolu asked questions and the soldier tried to explain. He pointed to himself and to the stripes sewn on his sleeves. "Sergeant!" he said.

He made it plain that the soldiers had been traveling through the country for many days and that they would be many more days on the trail. He and the soldiers with him were of the Kimboosie tribe, but they knew the American speech.

Momolu began to feel that the soldier's life was good. Soldiers traveled; they saw many people and many places.

The sergeant smiled as he talked. His hands waved and his expression changed swiftly in his eagerness to make himself understood. He was different, but somehow he was not so very different from the men of Lojay, Momolu thought.

The sergeant took off his round red cap and put it on Momolu's head, setting it well forward to one side. Everyone standing near exclaimed, and the sergeant laughed and clapped his hands. Then he took off his shirt and put that on Momolu, showing him how to close it down the front with bottons. He climbed out of his pants, and standing only in his loincloth, he helped Momolu into the pants and wound the wide blue sash about Momolu's waist. Then he sat down on the ground and took off the wraparound cloths from his knees to his ankles and wound them about Momolu's legs.

Now Momolu stood a full-dressed soldier. Those who saw laughed with glee and called to those who stood around other fires. They came and looked and ran back to summon still more friends. Soon Momolu was the center of a great crowd who pushed close to see him and called out.

"Momolu!" they said. "Momolu is no more a boy. He is a soldier. Momolu is a full man now!"

While Momolu was marching up and down, trying to look like a soldier, he heard Flumbo's angry voice, and his father pushed through the crowd.

"What!" Flumbo shouted at the sight. "My son

would go over to the enemy. Get out of it. Get out of it right now!"

Flumbo was very angry. He seized Momolu by the arm, and without stopping to unbutton the shirt, he tore it with one movement off Momolu's back. Then he ripped off the pants. Flumbo did not pull Momolu out of the pants; he pulled the pants away from his son, tearing them so badly that they would never be useful again.

The sergeant shouted. What he actually said Momolu did not know. The sergeant rushed at Flumbo, trying to save his clothes, but Flumbo, who was as strong as the soldier, pushed him back, so that he stumbled and fell into the bright burning fire.

In after days Momolu felt certain that the soldier had meant no harm, and of course he knew that his father was not a bad but a good man. But when the sergeant got up, he rushed at Flumbo with a roar like that of a wild animal, and the two men fought. The other men and Momolu tried in vain to part them. The sergeant called out, and more soldiers came. Not understanding, they thought their sergeant was being hurt, and soon all the men of Lojay were fighting against the soldiers.

Momolu was struck and pulled and shoved, and all the while he tried and tried to make the people stop fighting. They did not stop. Women screamed. Someone started beating the great drum in the palaver house. It was a call to war.

Momolu was knocked down. He saw a forest of legs above him. He rolled over and got to his feet, determined to get out of the fight. A sharp pain caught him on the jaw, and everything went black.

3

The sergeant did not sleep in Flumbo's house that night. The leader of the soldiers collected all his men from the homes of Lojay, and they and the sergeant slept in the shelter of the palaver house.

Momolu could hardly talk for pain, but Portee tried to explain to Flumbo that the sergeant and her son were only playing. She scolded her husband and put cold water on Momolu's swollen face and rubbed it with ointment of palm oil and pepper.

Early the following morning the people were summoned to the palaver house. Chief Logomo sat high in his great carved chair. He wore a blue silken robe with a round cap of the same cloth. His gold breastplate with the heavy chain sparkled in the morning light. His sword lay across his knees.

Behind him the old men of the council stood, each one bearing his ceremonial spear. Bomo-Koko with his own drummer and two lesser priests were at the chief's left. The leader of the soldiers, the one they called captain, sat at the chief's right with a low table before him. A leather bag for carrying papers was on the table near him and he was writing on a sheet of paper. Beside the table, the sergeant stood, dressed in fresh clothes, unsmiling and erect.

While they gathered taking their places, the men of Lojay scarcely spoke, or if they spoke, it was in low tones. Momolu had never sat in a big palaver before. He had always been outside with the women and other boys. Now he was at his father's side in the first row of those seated before the platform.

Bama was playing his drum softly. Chief Logomo lifted his hand, and the drum rapped loudly for silence, then settled back again to a slow, soft beat as Tinsoo, Chief Logomo's spokesman, stepped forward.

In his high, piping voice, old Tinsoo said that the people of Lojay had been called for a serious palaver. Wrong had been done. The darkness of hate was in the eyes of men. Justice would have to bring light.

Tinsoo was a man of great wisdom. He had traveled far. It was said he was able to speak with the people of every tribe. None remembered when any had come to Lojay whose speech Tinsoo did not know.

Chief Logomo spoke next. He spoke first in Kewpessie, saying that the hearts of the people of Lojay were not evil and that if they had done any wrong, they must now do those things that would make the wrong right. If the people of Lojay had been wrongly attacked, they should ask for a just settlement and for protection from evil men. Then turning to the captain, he spoke with him in the American tongue.

The captain stood, while Chief Logomo spoke. He smiled and bowed in agreement, and when he answered, wise Tinsoo stood before him, his head to one side, catching every word. It was Tinsoo who spoke the captain's word to the people.

"To the people of Lojay," he said, his words sharp and clear, "the captain brings greetings from the Liberian government. The captain says his heart is good for all the people of the country and he goes about with his soldiers only to protect the good people from those whose hearts are evil. So the captain says he came to Lojay. The captain says he does not understand how after the palaver of last night the men of Lojay fought against his soldiers. Now his heart cannot lie down. If the soldiers did the people of Lojay wrong, then the people must say, but if"—Tinsoo frowned and raised his finger in the air—"if the people of Lojay have hurt the soldiers without cause, then the government's heart will not lie down. So the captain says!"

Now Chief Logomo and the captain started hearing in turn those who were to tell their stories. The sergeant spoke first. Each thing the sergeant said in his speech, Tinsoo repeated in Kewpessie so that all could know whether he spoke the truth. The sergeant said that at first the people had been kind to him and he had been glad to be in such a happy town. Then Flumbo had come and broken up their little play without regard for either the value of the government's cloth or the dignity of himself, the government's trusted sergeant.

He showed the clothes Flumbo had torn. He showed the indignities done to his person. When he took off his pants to show where he was burned when Flumbo pushed him into the fire, the people stretched their necks to see, and when he said that he had been unable to sit down since, the people drew in their breath and murmured in sympathy.

Other soldiers came forward then. They showed their soiled or torn clothing. Some had swollen places on their faces, but of these they did not speak, for they were men and would not complain of small hurts. None of them were able to say how the fight had started. They had only answered when their sergeant called. They had only fought because others fought.

When it was Flumbo's turn to speak, Momolu's heart seemed to turn over. He could see that as his father went forward, Flumbo was trying hard not to limp on his stiff leg.

Chief Logomo asked Flumbo first if he would tell the truth as his father had taught him to know the truth. And after Flumbo said he would tell the truth, and that if he told a lie, his words would choke him and he would fall down before them all and die, Logomo told him to speak.

"I do not like soldiers," Flumbo began. "I have seen soldiers before this time, and I cannot open my heart to evil men who kill."

When Tinsoo told the captain what Flumbo had said, Momolu thought that the captain would be angry, but he only listened and bowed his head.

"As I myself would never march with soldiers," Flumbo went on, "I would not want to see my one son go with them. Now this sergeant says he was only making play with my son. So he says—but what sort of play is it that puts the cloth of government on Momolu's frame? What sort of play is that, but to make my one son love the feeling of being a soldier so that he will leave his father's house and go forth to kill?"

So Flumbo spoke, and he spoke more, about boys becoming men and leaving their homes and their part of the country to go to far places never to return. The men of Lojay turned each one to the other as he spoke, and each knew that Flumbo spoke with sense.

When Flumbo was through with his speaking, he took his place again beside Momolu and laid a hand upon the shoulder of his son.

The captain and the chief put their heads together. Momolu watched their faces. Neither seemed to be displeased. Only the sergeant looked stern and angry as he stood there, rigid and straight, looking out over the heads of the people. When the chief and the captain seemed to agree, Bama beat on his drum for silence.

"My people," said Logomo, "this is a bad thing that has been done. A man who knows all will do right, but what man can know all?" He clapped his hands together and turned them palms up, empty.

"It is well said," all the people cried.

"The captain comes to us in peace," Logomo went on. "His soldiers only make play with our people, but our brother Flumbo does not understand. He thinks only that he must save his son. For this, we cannot blame him."

Again all the people cried out together in agreement.

Logomo raised his hand. He gazed about at all the people, and then he turned to where Flumbo sat with Momolu beside him.

"The captain is a just man whose heart goes out to Flumbo and the people of Lojay. He holds nothing against a man who does not like soldiers.

He would not have Flumbo punished, but he would have him be a wiser man. Now the government has lost the clothes its soldiers wear, so Flumbo, whose swift anger brought the trouble, must pay ten bags of rice, and Flumbo with Momolu, his son, must take the rice to Cape Roberts on the coast and stand before the commissioner who is the captain's chief. This is the will of the captain, and this is the will of Logomo, chief of Lojay. The palaver is finished."

All the people started talking at one time, at first softly and then loudly. There was not one to say that it was not right, but ten bags of rice would be half the crop from Flumbo's harvest. His friends gathered about Flumbo, telling him that he should not worry, that all would help him. Old Tinsoo was one of the first. He held Flumbo's hand clasped in his while he spoke, and at the end as their hands separated the fingers popped.

No one looked at Momolu as he slipped away. The sun was shining. Birds were singing. Children were playing. The world about him was just the same as yesterday, but to Momolu everything seemed different; his heart was heavy.

Passing the house of Chief Logomo, he heard

his name called. He looked about. There was no one in sight. He thought it was just his imagination.

"Momolu!"

The voice was gentle. He stopped and took a step toward the chief's house. In the shadow of the open door stood Mah-Way, Dairku's younger sister.

"Never mind, Momolu. Let your heart lie down," she said. "You will go, but you will come again."

4

Momolu had never been to the coast.

In the quiet darkness just before the coming of day, he was riding in the front of the canoe while Flumbo paddled opposite him. His eyes searched the surface of the river ahead. A floating log or an early moving alligator could make trouble.

The chill of the night air reached under his robe and slid along his skin. He wanted to pull his blanket around his shoulders, but it was somewhere behind him. Crouching low, he shrugged himself down deeper into his robe.

It was quiet on the river. There was the splash of Flumbo's paddle and the thump as it came to rest against the hull of the dugout at the end of each stroke. Another canoe followed. The thump of Nisa-Way's paddle was like an echo. The soft thump of Flumbo's paddle, then the thump of Nisa-Way's, and the steady singing of sliding water under the bow and along the sides were the only sounds.

The two canoes had left Lojay early. Flumbo could have loaded all ten bags of rice in his own boat, but Nisa-Way, who was Flumbo's best friend, had come with his canoe to help, and the chief had said that old Tinsoo should go with them also. Tinsoo would speak for Chief Logomo when Flumbo and Momolu went before the commissioner.

Somewhere along the bank a pepper bird cried out. The pepper bird was the first of forest creatures to awaken.

"Day comes now!" Momolu called over his shoulder.

"Day comes now!" Flumbo's voice repeated.

"Day comes now!" "Day comes now!" came the voices of Nisa-Way and old Tinsoo in the canoe behind them.

Momolu remembered the old saying, "For every night a day." So it was. Trouble had come, and now Flumbo was forced to take his good rice to

Cape Roberts and stand before the government man. Yet if the trouble had not come, Momolu would never have had this chance to travel. Now he would see other people and learn the strange ways of foreigners.

In the early morning light they passed a cluster of houses on the right bank. Women were stirring around their fires. Men bathing in the shallows called out greetings. Momolu had often visited this village. He had friends here. He watched as the canoe passed and knew that if any of the boys recognized him they would envy him his trip to the outside world.

He looked back at his father. "Now I can paddle," he said.

Flumbo agreed. He shook the water from his paddle before he laid it across the bags of rice. As the canoe lost its speed Momolu, careful not to upset the balance, turned in his place and kneeled, facing Flumbo. With his own paddle he swung the dugout around, so that Flumbo's end pointed downstream. While they made the change, Nisa-Way's boat went by them.

Momolu had not realized how fast the two canoes were moving. Now he found it hard to keep

41

Nisa-Way from pulling far ahead. At first he timed his stroke by that of the other paddle. Soon the gap widened. He paddled faster. For a time it seemed that he was gaining. The sun was not yet high enough to reach them on the river, but Momolu was very warm. Without losing a stroke, he worked his robe up over his arms and over his head, and let it drop on the five bags of rice. The other canoe was far ahead, and yet Nisa-Way's paddle was moving not nearly so fast as Momolu's.

From his place in the forward end, Flumbo spoke. "If my son works so fast," he said, "he will not work so long. Let us work at this together."

Without taking up his paddle, Flumbo raised his hands and moved his arms as though he were truly working. He explained that Momolu's stroke was not long enough. He showed him how the body should swing with each motion, so that the back would do most of the pulling.

It was easy, Momolu found. The canoe made greater speed. "For true," he said, "I could paddle all day like this. See, we will soon be up to Nisa-Way now."

It took longer than Momolu had thought it

would, but the gap did close and Momolu did not become tired.

Where the Tamby-Oway River poured itself into a larger river, they reached Lamalla, the first large town. In the shallow water, men were fishing with nets.

Momolu had been to Lamalla before. Flumbo came here to trade his palm oil and nuts and piassava for cloth and iron pots and other things he needed. The trader at Lamalla was one of the few white men Momolu had ever seen.

Some of the people in Lojay thought that white people did not have any skin, but Flumbo had told Momolu that this was not so. Nevertheless, the first time Momolu saw the white trader he was afraid. He held tight to his father's robe and stood behind him while Flumbo talked with the man in his strange house filled with even stranger things from the far outside world. When the trader offered him candy, Momolu had not wanted to take it. He thought the white hand would be cold and damp like the underside of a lizard.

People from the town gathered on the bank as the two canoes headed for the shore. They were Kewpessies and friends of the people of Lojay.

Men and boys waded into the water and helped to work the canoes high on the sandy bank. Their backs bent low to old Tinsoo who rode with Nisa-Way. They spoke gently to him, but they laughed and popped fingers with Flumbo and Nisa-Way, and inquired about those they knew in Lojay.

They saw that in each canoe there were five bags of rice, and they looked from one to the other with questions in their eyes, but no one asked the visitors where they were going or why. It would be rude for the people of Lamalla to inquire.

Tinsoo, with an old councilor on each side, led the way through the town to the house of Lamalla's chief. Momolu saw the boys of the town watching him as he followed with Flumbo and Nisa-Way behind Tinsoo.

They faced the curtained door of the chief's square house. A small boy came from the house and placed a low stool in front of the door. The people of Lamalla stood about, talking among themselves while they watched.

Inside the house, a drum sounded. No one spoke as the curtain parted, and the chief came out with his head bowed low, as though searching for something on the ground. He took his seat and fanned himself delicately. It was as if he did not know that visitors waited before him and all the people of his town were watching.

Suddenly his head came up; his eyes widened; his lips parted in a shout. "What is this?" he asked as though surprised. "Does the oldest man of Lojay come to our humble village to stand in the sun?"

The small boy ran from the house, carrying a second stool which he placed on the ground in front of the chief.

Tinsoo bowed low and placed his right hand over his heart. "The wise chief of Lamalla," he said, "has a good heart for the servant of his friend, the chief of Lojay."

It took a long while to go through all the ceremonies of visiting, and Momolu was hungry. He shifted his weight from side to side, and knew that before it was finished, he would be very tired.

Tinsoo presented a fresh leopard skin as a gift from Chief Logomo. Then the whole story of the soldiers' visit had to be told. It was not war palaver, he explained, but it was like war.

When the chief replied, he said that his heart

turned over with sympathy, "One man's trouble is the trouble of all his brothers."

The men of Lojay must eat the food of Lamalla and rest themselves while the sun was high. When they left, they should know that the hearts of the people of Lamalla would not lie down until the men of Lojay should have returned safely to the Kewpessie country.

Momolu was more than ready to eat. He did not usually sleep in the day, but after his stomach was full, he lay down and slept without dreaming.

5

In the afternoon when they were on the river again, Flumbo seemed more cheerful than Momolu had seen him since the trouble started. The people of Lojay had told him not to worry. To have the friendship and kind words of the Kewpessie people of another town gave him even more comfort.

Flumbo had been to the coast before. He knew the river, the places of danger, the towns along the way where they would find welcome. Each year a party went to the coast to take the town's share of tax rice to the government.

"Hut tax!" the people would say as they brought their measure of rice to pile in the palaver house. "Hut tax for government so government can eat and send soldiers out so they can fight."

They said government must eat, but Momolu could not understand what the government might be or why the people of Kewpessie must feed it. Government was strong. Its men went through the land, and no chief or council or town could refuse to pay its share of tax.

Momolu had heard of how not one town alone but many towns of Kewpessie people had fought in war against the government. They had fought, but always more and more soldiers came, and those who died among the people were many. The soldiers burned the people's houses and took away their cattle and their women. Those who died among the soldiers were few. Yet still more and more soldiers came with guns until the country-side was filled with bobbing red caps and their shouts would make the hiding people cringe. The soldiers burned the towns, and the smoke filled the skies and shut out the sun and hid the stars at night.

Momolu had never seen such a war, but he had heard the stories the old men told of it. Their voices came husky from their throats in telling of the terror that had lived in Kewpessie country. Some would weep naming the fathers and the brothers who had gone with spears and swords to face the guns of government and die.

Storytellers too talked of war. There were two kinds of war they talked about—or maybe three, Momolu remembered.

First, there was the war of equals, war between the towns within a single tribe or war between tribes when the Kewpessies fought against the Krus or against the Golas. In such a war the men of one side would sweep into a town to kill with spears and drive off the cattle and steal the women if they could. While the Kewpessie men were striking at the towns of the Gola people, their own towns would be raided. Finally when one tribe had lost too much and found itself too weak to go on with the war, they would beg for peace, and with a great palaver, all the fighting would cease. People would rebuild their towns and mourn their dead. Then they would forget.

Momolu was paddling, while Flumbo lay back at ease with one hand trailing over the side in the water. He looked comfortable and not unhappy.

"Pa," Momolu said, "now my head thinks about

soldiers and government. Why do country people make war with government?"

Flumbo lifted his cupped hand and let the water trickle out over his chest.

"It is a senseless business," he said. "Government is of the Liberian people. They rule all the country where live the tribes of our Kewpessies, and of the Bassas, the Golas, the Krus, and many more. The Liberian people are strong. They follow the ways of white men, although they are not white. They have guns, and they know books. Small boys and even girls are taught to read and write. They know the magic of machines for motorcars and trucks, for boats and great ships, for planes that cross the skies, and for the radio."

There were no roads leading to Lojay, but Momolu had seen trucks when he visited other towns. Motorboats were often on the river, and he had heard the hum of planes and seen them flying high in the sky. The planes looked so small overhead that he believed the people who rode in them must have been changed by some magic power into creatures of the spirit world. It would take magic greater by far than any known to Bomo-Koko.

Truck, ship, plane, radio—all of these were words he knew. He had learned the words, but he did not understand them or how they worked. He had heard the magic box of radio. Most of the people of his town would run from the sounds, saying that evil spirits were in the air. He did not run from it. He too supposed that radio was a thing of magic, but he believed the spirits were not evil. He thought that they were surely good, happy and full of dancing

"The Liberians have a word for what they know," Flumbo said. "People who know books and have guns and understand machines call themselves civilized."

Civilized, it was not a new word to Momolu. He had heard it before. He nodded his head and kept paddling, hoping that Flumbo would go on.

"Government has a civilized way to make war." Flumbo shook his head from side to side. "It is not wise for those who are weak to fight against the strong."

"But why?" Momolu asked again. "Why do the people of the country fight against the government?"

Flumbo lifted his head. He was smiling. "Why

did your father fight against the sergeant in Lo-jay?" he asked

Momolu did not answer and Flumbo went on. "Our people do not like the ways of civilized Liberians," he said. "We do not like to see our sons put on their kind of clothes or take their way of living."

Not here, Flumbo said, but nearer the coast among the Krus they had often fought. The Kru people, closer to the outside world and living with Liberians, had fought with guns in the civilized way, yet they were never strong enough to win.

"Then there was another kind of war," Flumbo spoke more slowly. "There was another kind of war that does not come again. It was not a war between two tribes or of a country tribe against the higher government. No man would call it so. It was a war of the strong against the helpless and weak. It was not a war of hate but a war of fear."

This was the third kind of war of which the storytellers spoke, Momolu remembered, and as the tales were told, women would scream as though in pain and men would bow their heads and cry.

"Strong men came out of the north with guns

and spears and many lengths of hard iron chains. They wanted not so much to kill but to take the people. Old and young, men and women and little children, all the people they could get, they took them off to sell as slaves. At the coast they sold them. There white men came from far-off lands across the seas with ships, great boats bigger than any palaver house in all the land. The white men took our people to their country to work their farms and build their houses. Our people never came again. It was long ago, but it was war."

Momolu rested his paddle while he thought of the people taken from towns like Lojay and Lamalla and other towns that he had seen. He wondered what he would have done had white strangers taken him away to their land across the sea.

"What of those people taken long ago?" he asked. "Why did not our people go to bring them back? If every tribe of our people should unite, could we not have our brothers return?"

Flumbo shook his head. "My son forgets that slavers took our people long time past, too long ago. Those people are dead. Their children too are dead. It was in the olden days. Word comes to our country that in far America black men have joined with white men to make the strongest nation in the world. In that land all the people live the American way. The children of our brothers are many. They call America their homeland. Some of them cross the seas to our African shore, but they are not like us. They think we are the strangers, the wild ones like monkeys in the bush.

"Some have come to stay on the shore, and you will see them. At Cape Roberts you will see them in the houses they learned to make in far America. They wear the clothes of that land. Pants cover their legs and shoes their feet. They know books. They are civilized. They are the ones we call Liberians."

"They are strong, the Liberians," Momolu said.

"For true! They are strong for true." Flumbo shook his head. "In olden days the men who made their war for slaves, they too were strong. They knew the book palaver. They traveled. Does strength make good?"

Flumbo took up his paddle. He swung the canoe so that the bow became the stern and the stern the bow. He set himself to work with long swift strokes. Nisa-Way's canoe was far ahead.

6

In the late afternoon of the second day, the two canoes were drawn up on the bank of a town in Gola country. Tinsoo knew well the speech of the Golas and even Flumbo and Nisa-Way could make themselves understood, for many Gola and Kewpessie words were nearly the same. It was said that the Kewpessie and Gola were brother tribes, but Momolu, among them for the first time, felt himself a foreigner.

He watched with wonder in his eyes. They did not look like his people. They did not look altogether different, but somehow they were not the same. Momolu saw boys who were the same size and probably the same age as he. They watched him, and they talked together among themselves, but they did not come near or speak to him. Momolu decided he did not like them.

While old Tinsoo went alone to pay his respects to the town's chief, the others set about building a fire near the palaver house to cook in their own pots their rice and dried fish and palm oil.

Momolu remembered how in Lojay he had watched with the other boys while strangers did their cooking in his town. He had laughed at the things they did and the way they spoke. Now he smiled and said to Flumbo, "The Gola people think we are funny."

"Every man is thought a monkey when he is in a foreign land," Flumbo said. "So it is, but wait until you come to the Kru coast. You yourself will feel like a monkey."

Momolu laughed. "That will be good," he said. "When I was a small boy I used to try to think how it would feel, if I were a monkey, to swing by my tail. Now it seems that I will finally know."

Flumbo became serious. He leaned forward and spoke softly. His eyes narrowed as he said, "You have heard the mystery of the white man? He has a tail, and that is why he must wear long pants on his legs. They hide his shame."

Momolu had heard this said but never by his father. His own eyes widened in surprise. Then he saw Flumbo's face break into a smile, and knew that it was a joke; his father had only been fooling him. But why, he asked himself, why did the white man wear such clothes? It was still a mystery.

They slept that night in the shelter of the palaver house, and in the morning the Gola people's chief sent word that they should take their morning meal with the people of the town. Each was led to a different house.

Momolu remembered how friendly the sergeant had been to him at his father's house in Lojay. He tried to act like the sergeant. True, he had no clothes to put on anyone, but he played with the children, and he tried to talk with the men. When he ate, he tried to make the women know that their food was good. He told them their roasted plaintains were the best he had ever tasted. It was not true, but he told himself that it was really not a lie either because they did not understand his words.

As a small boy, Momolu had been skillful in standing on his hands and walking about with his feet high in the air. It had been a long time since he had tried the trick, but he wanted to do something for the joy of these kind people and their children. Twice he tried and failed. Then with a short run he threw his hands down hard and kicked his feet into the air. He poised and steadied himself. Then one hand went out to take a step, another, and another. So he moved; so he walked. The men shouted their praise; the women clapped their hands. The children danced and crowded around him in their delight. When he was tired and had righted himself, they called for more, repeating over and over the same few words until they formed a chant. His heart warmed within him, and until the others were ready to leave, he did his trick again and again, joining in the people's laughter and glee.

It was only when the two canoes were about to draw away from the shore that he learned the meaning of the Gola people's words. He was waving to them while they danced on the beach, repeating their call. Then shame fell on his head; Flumbo told him what they were saying:

Monkey man!
Monkey man!
Turn your tail up in the sky!
O you monkey man!

At midday and again that evening when they stopped at other Gola towns, Momolu tried hard not to look or act like a monkey. His ear was alert for the word. It was not spoken.

7

~~~~~~

On the fourth day Flumbo said, "Tonight we will sleep in Kru country. Civilized Liberians live there too. This river will lead us into another, which the Liberians call the Dunbar. Our people call it the Ever-Hungry."

"Is it the alligators in the waters?" Momolu asked. "Is it the alligators who seize on men that give the waters such an evil name?"

"Not so," his father said. "I have told you of the time when strong men took our people to the coast to sell for slaves. So that they could not escape, they fastened our people with chains. They watched them on the trail and beat them so our people could not fight or stop to die. Sometimes they brought the captives in canoes by water, or if by land, they had to cross the river. The Kewpessie people upset their boats in the wide deep waters of the Ever-Hungry. The masters could not stop them. Weighted down with heavy chains, they died. Their spirits live in the water still. Now the spirits vex and twist the boats of those who do not please them. I myself have seen canoes that were well loaded and even, riding with no thought of danger, suddenly turn up and over."

"Then should we not make a sacrifice to please the spirits?" Momolu asked.

"For true," Flumbo replied. "Tinsoo will know the words to say, and he has brought gifts prepared by Bomo-Koko."

"I hope those poor ones will be content," said Momolu.

He was not thinking of the danger to himself. He and Flumbo were both good swimmers; it was the rice he thought of; they could not let anything happen to the rice. On the river at Lojay at play with the other boys, it was great sport overturning a canoe. In the water they would gather at one side and with a heave turn the dugout right side up; then when the water was spilled from the hull by rocking, they again would climb aboard.

An upset boat was fun at home, but it would not be sport to lose their precious cargo. Besides, Momolu did not want to disturb the spirits of those brave ones who had died in their own waters rather than live as slaves across the sea.

"We will be on the Ever-Hungry, but we will not pass over the water people's place," Flumbo said. "Old Tinsoo knows. He will take the paddle, and he will lead. We will follow the way he takes. It will not be as straight, but in so doing, we will not disturb the spirits, and they will be at peace."

During the last four days, they had been on as many rivers. Each had widened as their paddling took them farther and farther downstream. In the afternoon the canoes entered a section where water rushed swiftly between and over and around great rocks. Momolu rested while Flumbo handled the canoe, proving his skill with every stroke, avoiding the shallows and finding the right channel, speeding through swift rapids where the dugout might have smashed or turned over onto the rocks.

It was late in the afternoon when Momolu saw his first Liberian town. Where the canoes reached

the Ever-Hungry River, a double row of houses
stood, beyond the far bank, on the hill. Their
straight white walls were topped with roofs
painted red. Flumbo explained that they were
built to look like American houses. Their walls
were made of stone or sun-baked brick or sheets of
corrugated iron nailed to wooden frames. All the
roofs were made of iron brought from across the
sea. They were large houses with wide porches,
and many windows standing open to the breeze.

The homes of the African people were closer to
the waterside. They were more like houses in Lojay, though some were made like the Liberian
houses on the hill. As the canoes drew nearer, Momolu saw that these houses were not well kept,
and the town itself was dirty. The thatch on the
roofs was thin, and in some places sheets of iron
had been used as patches. The clay walls were
marked with strange figures. A few had been
painted white, but this was long ago, for most of
the white had been washed off by the rains and the
brown mud showed through.

As the dugouts approached the beach, the people came down to the waterside. They stared as if
the men from Lojay were indeed monkeys, and

they laughed and pointed. Momolu stared back. He did not laugh. He did not feel that he was strange. It was the others who were strange. They looked dirty, and their town was dirty, and over it hung a dirty smell.

None of these people of the Kru tribe wore the simple clothes of upcountry people. Most of the men wore pants—short pants or long pants—and some of the pants were long in one leg and short in the other. Shirts or jackets of one kind or another covered the upper part of their bodies. On their heads some wore hats, not straw hats like the one old Tinsoo sometimes wore to save his bald head from the sun, but smooth cloth hats with flopping brims or round caps with peaks in front. Most surprising of all, some of the men wore figured wraparounds like those that the women in Lojay wore. Momolu had to look hard to be sure that they were men. It was hard to understand.

The people laughed among themselves, but they were not friendly. No man waded out to help the Kewpessie men send their dugouts high on the sandy beach. They only watched and laughed, until the man who seemed to be their chief came to the waterside and shouted something at them and waved the men of Lojay off.

Momolu was not sorry he should not stay among such people. The two canoes backed away and turned and headed downstream where they found a place to go ashore. It was quiet and it was clean. They could not see or smell the ugly town.

While their pots bubbled over the fire, they washed in the river. That night they slept in their canoes, stretched out on the bags of rice.

"These people are so-so rogues," old Tinsoo said.

Before he fell asleep, Momolu wondered if the water here was clean. He still felt dirty.

8

The two canoes were on the water the next morning before the sun got up. It would be the last day of the journey to the coast. Their progress was good, for the current was swift. Many other canoes were on the river. They were larger than the boats of upcountry people. And also on the river were motorboats moving swiftly with steady roaring sounds. The people who rode in them seemed happy, not fearful at all. Momolu was trying to figure it out in his mind when he saw something even more strange. A huge white boat, different from anything he had ever seen before, pulled away from a town on the bank. It was bigger than any house Momolu had ever seen. Behind it a boiling streak marked its path.

"Steamboat" Flumbo said. "It is like a ship that moves by fire, but it is not so large. Your eyes will see!"

The winding course they followed took them close by an evil-smelling place, and the stench was in Momolu's nostrils. He wondered if the others smelled it too. Then his father turned, and he saw that Flumbo had wrinkled up his nose and was frowning.

"Does strength make good?" Flumbo asked.

Momolu knew that his father was wise. The coast was not good, but from what he was now seeing, Momolu doubted if these people even had strength.

Later as they passed a larger town, a bell was ringing. It made a pleasing sound as it floated to them across the water. Momolu held his paddle quiet to listen.

"Mission!" Flumbo pointed to the hill beyond the town where a group of white houses stood apart. People were moving about, most of them children wearing white clothing. When the pealing of the bell was ended and lost in silence, the children formed a line and filed two by two into the door of the largest house where the sign of the

Christians, a large white cross, was mounted on the roof.

Flumbo said, "The people who make the missions take the children of our people. They take them in and make them live in the American way. As the little ones grow in the new way, they forget the country life. When they are full men and women, they live with Liberians. They are lost to us."

"Why then do our people let the missionaries have their children?" Momolu could not see why Africans should want to live like other people. "Do not the chiefs and wise men of the council try to save the little ones?"

"Who can say?" Flumbo lifted his shoulders. "Who can say whether it is better to have a son leave altogether or grow up to live in dirty towns like we saw last night?"

"But they could leave." Momolu felt sure of that. "They could leave and go farther up the river where the towns are clean and people live in friendship."

"What a man knows is good to him. What he does not know he fears. People of the bush country come to the coast to trade, to bring rice and other things for government. Sometimes they stay. People of the coast need never go to the bush. They do not know it, and so they fear the bush country. They know only their own way of life. Sometimes they think that it is bad, but they do not know where they might find better."

"Now I have seen." Momolu was satisfied. "And I know our life is better. I would never leave it."

Flumbo smiled. "Wait," he said. "You cannot judge by what you see in one day from the water-side or by what you smell. Let your heart lie down. Your mouth may yet sing another song."

Cape Roberts was another song, indeed.

Momolu was not prepared for such a sight. He had never before known a thrill like the one he felt when his eyes first looked on the town that was Cape Roberts. The Ever-Hungry River, wide and smooth, bespoke of nothing evil. The course all through the day had veered first to one side, then to the other. Now in cool shadows they skirted on the left around a bend. Across the silver water stretching ahead around the bend, the land was high.

71

Momolu was paddling. His chief task was to steer so that they followed along the way that Nisa-Way led, for the current bore the canoes swiftly.

The leading canoe rounded the bend, and Momolu heard a cry. His paddle dug deep and his arms strained; then he swung into full view of the city on the opposite bank.

White and red, the buildings mounted up from the bank in even rows, and on the highest point, a white cross glistened bravely in the rosy evening light. Palm trees raised their tufted heads along the line of sky. At the foot of the hill, just above the water's edge, a nest of native houses huddled on the beach. All the colors—the white, the greens, the reds, the soft tans of mud walls—took on the glow of the red ball of sun that hovered low above the wide stretch of water that was the open sea.

It was too far to see any dirt that was there. It seemed as if every house in such a place must be well kept and every person kindly and happy. These people would have strength, and they would be good. All that Momolu saw before him was beautiful. For a time he stared in blank amazement.

As one who dreams and by some magic finds his dreaming world is all about him in real life, Momolu's body became alive. His paddle shot from his hands high into the air. His heart, his soul, leaped up. He rose to his feet; his fingers quivered high overhead. A song came from his throat, and when it was ended, he bowed himself as though in prayer. He bowed and raised himself, and bowed again.

Flumbo took up his paddle. Sure swift strokes turned the canoe to where Momolu's paddle floated on the water.

The dugout swung sharply. Flumbo cried out in alarm. "Water people!"

Momolu heard his father's cry as he felt the hull sway beneath his feet. He tried to get his balance, but the dugout was tilting dangerously. Nisa-Way shouted from his canoe. For one dizzy moment Momolu was falling, and then he was in the water, the canoe floating bottom upward, its sleek underside looking like the belly of a sea monster.

9

Everything in the canoe was lost.

"It was the water people," said those of Kru Town who watched from the shore.

"Fool!" said Nisa-Way to Flumbo. "You are my friend, Flumbo, but your son is a double fool. Let me have him. I will beat him for you. I will make him know what it is to dance in a canoe."

Flumbo shook his head. "And what good will that do? Will you beat five bags of rice out of his back?" he asked.

That night Momolu sat in the dark, his back against the mud wall of Jalla-Malla's house in Kru Town. Around an outdoor table the men sat eating their rice and stew, but Momolu was not hungry. His heart had swelled so within him that there was no room for food.

He closed his eyes and seemed to feel again the swift lurch of the canoe beneath his feet. He had been frightened at that moment, not for himself but for the five precious bags of rice.

Flumbo had been very angry in the water. He had shouted loud harsh words, and when they tried to swing the overturned canoe to turn it right side up, Momolu had been excited. He did not do his part well. It was a struggle for father and son to get the dugout righted and cleared of water. Nisa-Way had pulled up close, and though he could not help, he added his scolding and raised his paddle as though to bring it down on Momolu's bobbing head.

Others had paddled out from shore. They had laughed, but they had helped, too. When at last Momolu and Flumbo were safe again inside their canoe, a motor launch was there, and the man in the stern threw a rope for Flumbo to hold. With much popping of its machine, the launch towed to the beach the floundering smaller boat.

Momolu had expected to be happy when they reached the coast. He had thought he would enjoy this first night among strange people in a strange land. Now, as he sat and watched the others eat, he had no hope of joy or pleasure in anything that he might do.

The sound of drums was in the air, but louder than the drums were the voices of radios. It seemed that every house in Kru Town had one of the magic boxes. Jalla-Malla's hung under the thatched eaves at the front of his house. The music that came from it was as strange to Momolu's ears as the words it spoke. He did not understand it. He was not cheered by it. He did not like it.

A lantern burned brightly on the long table. Night-flying insects swung in circles around the light, in spite of the palm-leaf fan waved by a girl standing beside Jalla-Malla's seat. A woman was bringing hot food from the fire to the table. Jalla-Malla was urging the others to eat. He said they had nothing to worry about, that he himself knew the government people. He would speak for his Kewpessie brothers and the government would hear him.

Jalla-Malla was a Kewpessie man who had come to the coast some years ago. Now he had a Kru woman for his wife, and in his house were small boys and girls who spoke the language of the Krus. As others came into the circle of the lantern's light, he called to them in Kru. They were his friends and neighbors, he said. In everything they treated him as a brother. He lacked only the black tattoo in the center of his forehead that marked all true members of the Kru tribe.

"But where is the boy?" Jalla-Malla asked, looking around the table.

Momolu did not want to join them. At home he was thought to be too young to sit with his father and the men who were his father's friends. He had come on the trip, hoping to play a man's part. He knew that he had failed.

Flumbo turned and peered into the darkness, calling Momolu's name.

A place was made on the bench for him to sit. Jalla-Malla smiled and called upon the woman, his wife, to bring another dish. Nisa-Way frowned and spoke of an empty head, but Flumbo nodded for Momolu to come forward.

Momolu thought he would be unable to eat, but as the others went on with their talk, he tasted the food and found it good.

Jalla-Malla was talking about his life in Kru Town.

"In our country upriver we have only one tongue, and every man needs to know only the Kewpessie speech," he said. "On the coast we have many tongues, and every man knows his own and others too."

Kru Town, he explained, was so called because most of the people who lived there were Kru. There were many such towns placed next to the towns of Liberians, who lived as the people of America lived in their country far across the sea. In Kru Town all the people could speak the American tongue. When they went into the town of Cape Roberts, they did their work and did their trading and talked their palavers with government men in the American speech.

The men of Kru Town were seamen who went aboard the great ships of the white men to work, moving cargo and stoking fires which gave the ships the power to move. Jalla-Malla had been on such ships for the space of many moons traveling to foreign shores.

"The great world is far more wonderful and strange than our upcountry people dream," he said.

Momolu forgot about his own troubles. He sat

listening, gazing around him with wide eyes, trying to understand all Jalla-Malla was saying.

"The things I could tell you about those lands, you would not believe. Me, I have seen them. I have seen other cities on the shore of Africa. In some of them the black men from many tribes are strong and free, and they make their own government. In others white men are strong, and the Africans, though they are many, are like slaves.

"I have seen white men in their own lands where black men are strangers, and where small boys and girls—yes, women, too—look on a black man and think he is a funny animal. In the white man's country it is cold, so cold that all the cloth a man can put over his skin will not keep him warm."

Flumbo leaned forward. "Is it true, Jalla-Malla?" he asked. "Is it true that in those countries the coldness makes the moving water still and hard like iron?"

Momolu thought his father foolish to ask such a question. He had heard a storyteller speak of such coldness, but he thought it was a tale of long ago and not of any land that Jalla-Malla might have seen.

Jalla-Malla bent his head and looked into his dish. "You will not believe me." His voice was low, and he was very solemn. "You will not believe me, as I did not believe before these eyes had seen it. It is true. As I am your Kewpessie brother, it is true. And may my eyes be darkened from this time and may my hands drop from me if my mouth is lying, I have seen the water hard like iron so that men walked upon it and so that a ship with all its power of fire could not move."

Long after they had finished with their food, they sat talking. Momolu had never heard anyone speak with such knowledge as this man from his own Kewpessie country. It was hard to believe that Jalla-Malla was like Flumbo and Nisa-Way and those who lived in Lojay.

"Yourself, Flumbo," Jalla-Malla said, "yourself could come to Kru Town and live as we live here. You would see and you would know."

Momolu looked at his father and saw him shake his head from side to side.

"No, my brother," Flumbo said slowly. "It is not for a man who has his house and his wife and his farm and all his life in Lojay. It is not for me." He raised his eyes to meet Momolu's gaze. "It is not for the old but for the young to leave the life they know and go to search for new ways, for life in strange lands."

"You have sense," Jalla-Malla agreed. "In Lojay all the people have one life, and every son follows in the footsteps of his father. Here we live many ways, and our sons choose each one the way that he will live, and the sons do not choose to follow the way of the fathers.

"My own son goes each day to the mission on the hill. There he learns the book. He learns the God palaver. By and by he will be what we call civilized. He will live with the Liberians. He will wear their clothes, and some day he will live in a house of iron and have for his wife a woman who will wear shoes."

"Then he will be lost!" It was Tinsoo's high-pitched voice. "Your son will be lost, and when you are old, he will not be with you. Why do you not keep him by your hand?"

"My son will be lost to life in Kru Town." Jalla-Malla nodded his head in agreement. "He will be lost to our way, but it can be that he will not forget his father. Some of the sons do forget and go far away and never return, but many who live among the Liberians walk with pride and make their old ones' hearts lie down. The young ones grow rich and give their fathers a better life than any they have ever known before. So it will be with John, son of Jalla-Malla."

Jalla-Malla got to his feet and turned into his house. Soon he came again, pushing before him his oldest son. The boy was tightening a blanket about his waist as he moved toward the table. Momolu guessed that he was eight or ten years old. In one hand he held a book.

Jalla-Malla said something to him in Kru. The small one shook his head and rubbed his eyes to get himself awake. Turning aside from the table, he held the book high so that light from the lantern should fall on its pages.

Strange sounds came from the small one's lips. He shouted his words in a clear voice, his finger moving along the lines of small black marks. Surely this boy who lived by the sea was cleverer than any Momolu had ever seen.

Momolu rose and walked around the table to stand beside the lad the better to see the wonder. There was a picture in the book. A boy with long yellow hair rode a horse; another boy walked beside him. John, son of Jalla-Malla, turned the page. Here there was no picture, but John's voice went on without pause, his finger moving steadily across and down the page. Momolu had no doubt that the boy was uttering the message of the book. He had never before seen a boy who knew book palaver.

Jalla-Malla spoke again to his son. The book was closed, and John asked something of his father. Jalla-Malla nodded. The small shoulders straightened. The face was turned upward toward the stars. John sang.

Sweet and soft and clear the voice came from him, his young body swaying gently. When it was over, he bowed to his father and then bowed low to those at the table. Jalla-Malla patted his shoulder and sent him back to his rest.

"I do not know the words the small one sang." Tinsoo's voice was soft too. "It was like the love songs of young girls in the gree-gree. What was it?"

"For true," Jalla-Malla smiled. "It was a love song for true. It was a mission song, and it was about the love of God. It says that God loves all

the children of the world. He loves the white ones just as much as the black ones. So the song says."

"O my father!" Momolu was eager as he looked at Flumbo. "I must go to mission. I must learn the book. Before we go back, you must take me to the mission on the hill so I too can learn the magic of the book."

Jalla-Malla shook his head. "It is not a thing for days or for moons. It is a thing for years," he said. "First you would have to learn the American talk, and then, after you knew it well, then you would study the book. It is a palaver of years."

Momolu bowed his head. He would have to go back to Lojay. He would never understand these mysteries.

"But you will be able to see this thing for yourself." Jalla-Malla added. "Tomorrow will be the day called Sunday when all the people, young and old, can go to mission. On Sunday we cannot see the government man for our own palaver. We will go to mission.

"Now it is late. We must sleep. Morning will come all too soon. At Cape Roberts there are many things for your eyes to see and your ears to hear. Your mouth will be full of things to tell when you go again to Lojay."

Later as Momolu, wrapped in a borrowed blanket, lay on a borrowed mat in Jalla-Malla's house, he was too excited to fall asleep. Then he remembered about the lost five bags of rice, and shame was upon him. Finally he slept, but his sleep was full of dreaming.

10

On the morning of the day that was called Sunday, Jalla-Malla led his visitors up the hill to Cape Roberts mission, along with his wife and son. Most of the others climbing the long steep path ahead of them and behind them were women dressed in their best cloth. Jalla-Malla's Kru woman wore a white blouse, sewn with colored thread in fine stitches to make designs of flowers and palm trees and bright birds, and a dark blue wraparound which reached from her waist down to her sandaled feet. In the blue cloth were great white splashes like stars, and twinkling in the white stars were smaller stars of red and green and yellow. On her head she wore a yellow turban, shining and golden in the sun.

It was plain to see that Jalla-Malla was rich. In his three-room house his woman had a box of clothes, and on her arms gold bracelets made clinking music, and from her ears hung other things of gold.

Jalla-Malla wore long pants of khaki cloth, and tight over his upper body, he wore a white knitted, short-sleeved shirt. His hat was white, a helmet such as traders wore.

Momolu felt himself strange, for he too was wearing pants. His robe was in the river. It had been too short for his long body, so he was not too sorry it was gone, and Jalla-Malla had given him a white knitted shirt and the pants, the first he had ever owned.

Flumbo had borrowed a robe from Jalla-Malla. Much like the one he had lost in the river, it hung from shoulder to knee. "I don't need pants on me," he told Momolu.

On the level place at the top of the hill the mission grounds and buildings were like a small town. A long white house of corrugated iron was in the center. The walls were white, but the roof was painted red. A screened porch stretched across the front. African girls in white dresses were passing in and out, and when Momolu heard them speak, he did not understand their words, for all used the American speech.

Jalla-Malla told him about the houses and what they were used for. In the large house the missionaries, the white man and his woman, made their home. Some of the rooms were filled with seats, and on the walls were pictures and great squares of black. Classes of boys and girls met there for instruction. There were two floors in the house. Girls slept on the upper level, each one in her own American-style bed. Beyond and to the right were two smaller houses for boys.

Jalla-Malla led Momolu and his friends to let them look inside. Down the middle, lanterns hung from the ceiling over long wooden tables. Books in neat piles were on the tables. Clothes hung from pegs along the walls, and under each peg leaned a rolled-up sleeping mat. Above the pegs were shelves holding more books and boxes and blankets.

"Before they go to sleep at night, the boys study their books here at the tables." Jalla-Malla explained.

Behind the larger house an open shed with an

iron roof sheltered two long tables. At one end huge kettles rested over a fireplace built of rocks, and overhead a row of smaller pots and pans glowed brightly. Momolu thought they were made of tin, but Jalla-Malla said the silver metal was called aluminum.

"It is good to see," Flumbo said, "but should we not go where the others are? See, they are going into the palaver house."

Jalla-Malla agreed. "We will not find a place if we wait," he said. "But it is not a palaver house. It is called a church in the American speech, and it is like a prayerhouse in the country."

The loud clang of a tolling bell made Momolu jump. It was followed by another clang and then another. A mission boy was swinging on the rope of a bell mounted high in a wooden frame. It was such a bell as Momolu had heard some days ago on the river. All the people in Cape Roberts must be able to hear the sound of it as it rang loudly out from the hilltop.

Momolu's heart was beating so hard when they entered the church that he thought all could have heard it had not the bell been ringing. This would be something to tell to Dairku when he again saw him in Lojay.

The inside of the church was indeed not unlike a palaver house. It was a huge rectangle with a high thatched roof and a raised platform at one end. The people sat on benches—the men on one side of the middle aisle and the women on the other—but strangely it was the older people who sat in back, the boys and girls who filled the front. It was something like waiting for the storyteller at home, but it was different, too. Here there was no drum. It was queer to see so many people sitting quietly with no drum sounding.

Momolu sat very still with Jalla-Malla on one side and Flumbo on the other. Tinsoo, being an old man of position and dignity, had gone with Nisa-Way as near the front as possible. He did not seem to notice that none of the other old men were near him. In Kewpessie country, even in a strange town, he would have been entitled to a place of honor.

The white missionary man walked down the aisle to the platform and turned and lifted his hands. Men and women bent their heads and closed their eyes. Wanting to be like the others, Momolu bowed his head too, but he did not close his eyes. He wanted to see. Though he did not understand the words, he knew the missionary was making a prayer to his god.

The missionary threw his head back, his long arms reached upward as though he were begging for help. He looked as if he might be sick or weak from hunger, but his voice was strong and clear and loud enough to reach far above the roof of the church.

The woman missionary sat with her head bowed at one side of the platform. She was different from her husband, for she was fat and her hair, light in color like dry rice straw, was coiled in a knot and piled on top of her head. She sat before a glistening wooden box like a table, and when the man was through with his praying, she put her fingers on the box. As she moved them, the box itself began to sing. Momolu started to rise to get a better look, but Flumbo laid a hand on his knee, and Jalla-Malla leaned over and said, "It is called an organ. In a minute we will rise and sing."

Then all the people stood up and started to sing such a song as little John had sung the night before. On the platform the tall lean white man began to move from side to side, not stepping far with his feet but waving his long arms. It was like a ceremonial dance of the Kewpessie people. As he moved he sang, and all the people sang out louder. Jalla-Malla joined in the song, and all about, the people sang and clapped their hands in time and stamped their feet on the ground.

Momolu heard not a word he knew, but the clapping of hands and stamping of feet were actions he understood. His hands came together. His feet beat on the floor. His body swung in time to the music, and in his heart he lost his feeling of strangeness and fear.

When the singing ended, the missionary read something from a book, and then he talked. Momolu had thought the white man might be sick or weak from hunger, but as he listened and watched, he knew he had been mistaken.

The man was strong and full of energy. He talked, sometimes softly as though he were begging the people to do something for him, sometimes loudly as though he were giving orders. He shouted and waved his arms and pointed his finger and made a fist and beat on the high table before him. Louder and louder he shouted his words, and the people seemed pleased. Some of them nodded their heads too, and clapped their hands together, and cried out as though they said in their own speech, "I agree! I agree!"

When the missionary was through with his part a young African man rose to take his place. He was of the Kru people, for down the middle of his forehead the tattoo showed black against his dark-brown skin. He read from the same book, but by some magic he read from it in the Kru tongue. Then he talked in Kru, shouting not so loud as the white man had shouted, but even more of the people seemed to understand what he said. They answered back with loud cries of "Aha!" and sucked in their breath and nodded their heads in approval.

Then there was more singing. The missionary woman played her organ, and all the people stood to sing. Young men passed small baskets down the rows, and people took out their money and put it in the baskets. Momolu had no money. He had never owned a piece of money in his life. Jalla-Malla put a hard brown piece into his hand, and when the basket came his way Momolu parted with his first and only and last penny. His heart did not lie down.

After the church palaver was over, Jalla-Malla greeted his friends. Momolu stood alone, watching the people, while the men of Lojay talked with others who were there from Kewpessie country. And as he stood there, he remembered another time when he was a smaller boy and he had stood alone.

It had been four years ago, and he had been with his father and mother in Barga Town. There was a great gathering of people, more people than he had ever seen before, and yet in all that crowd with his father laughing and talking with his friends, and his mother somewhere with the women, Momolu had been lonely. Now it was just the same. That other time he had found a friend of his own age. The other boy had been lonely too, but on that day they had become big friends, closer than Kewpessie brothers.

No other boy in this place seemed to be alone. There were many boys—some his own size and age—but they talked together and laughed at their own jokes and held themselves erect in their clean American kind of clothes. Some did not have the mark of the Kru people on their fore-head. Perhaps among them there might be a lad from Kewpessie country. Momolu did not want to seem to watch them, but he moved closer to them as though he were just walking by. As he passed, someone spoke to him. It was the young man who had read from the book and talked to the people in Kru.

He was much older than Momolu; he wore long pants and a jacket and on his feet were shoes.

"I can't understand your speech," Momolu said, but he stopped and smiled his thanks to one who had been kind to a stranger.

The young man said something else to him.

"I am Momolu, son of Flumbo, whose house is in Lojay in Kewpessie country." It was all that Momolu could tell him.

"Kewpessie?" The young man repeated. Then he turned and said something that sent one of the boys away.

Others gathered around to see the stranger. They were smiling, but Momolu did not think they were laughing at him, and so he did not mind.

Another boy pushed through the crowd and

stood before him. For a moment Momolu thought he was looking at a boy from Lojay, but no, that could not be. There was no one in Lojay who looked quite like this, and yet something familiar about his face reached into Momolu's thought.

"They told me that a visitor was here from Kewpessie country," the other boy said. "Now I have come to see, and for true, your face is like the face of one I have seen before, and you must be a brother Kewpessie."

"It is so!" Momolu was happy to meet a Kewpessie boy of his own age, and indeed this one seemed already an old friend. He repeated again his name and his father's name and the name of his town.

At this the Kewpessie boy sprang forward, laughing. Seizing Momolu by the shoulders, he shook him, and throwing his arms about him, he hugged him. He called to the others and laughed and talked, but all in American speech. Momolu was glad he was happy, but he did not understand. Everybody was talking but Momolu, and more and more people came to see the excitement.

Finally the boy spoke again in Kewpessie to Momolu alone. "You are indeed my friend and my brother," he said. "For so we pledged together when we were small boys in Barga Town. Together we saw our sisters at the gree-gree palavers. You put your fine red cap upon my head."

Both boys had changed and grown since they had shared the pleasures of that exciting day four years ago. The boy's country name was Birmah, but he said that now he was called David, which was the name of a great king of olden times.

With David speaking for him, Momolu became acquainted with the other mission boys. The missionary proved to be a kindly man who wanted Momolu to stay at the Cape Roberts mission and learn as David was learning.

Momolu did not fully explain to David why he had come with Flumbo on this trip to the coast. It was an unpleasant thought, and everybody was so cheerful that he did not want to spoil the happy feeling. Besides he himself had almost forgotten. Lojay seemed far away, and the soldier palaver was something that his friend could not help.

11

Momolu walked behind his father and the others as they moved slowly up the wide street in the town of Cape Roberts. Around him the people of the town were hurrying about their own affairs. A few were dressed in the simple clothes of the country, but most of the African people showed by their clothes that they were learning to live as Liberians. The men wore pants and shirts, and some were fully dressed with hats on their heads and shoes on their feet. A few white people moved among the others.

Momolu was too unhappy to enjoy the wonders of the stores and the noisy wrangling of the women who spread their wares on mats or low tables along both sides of the street. The stores were one and two stories high with wide open fronts to make it easy for those who wanted to buy to step in from the paving stones of the sidewalk. Fancy-colored cloth and shiny kettles and cooking-ware hung on rods suspended from the ceiling. On the back shelves rows and rows of cans showed what they contained by the bright pictures on their paper wrappings. There were hoes and shovels, and axes and knives, and many things for working on the farm and in the garden. There were many things, too many, that Momolu could not name or even guess how they might be used.

Radios were blasting their sounds over the air. It seemed that they were in every shop. In one place guns were hanging in a rack. Momolu wondered if just anyone who had money could buy them. If so, he thought, the people of the Kru tribe, having money and knowing how to use it, could arm themselves to fight.

This was the morning of the day after Sunday. Jalla-Malla had said that the day before Sunday was the real market day in Cape Roberts. Momolu could not imagine a more lively market than the one he saw now.

An old man in a Fantee robe was arguing over

the price of a leaf of tobacco on the table of a Kru woman. A white woman was selecting a chicken from the basket of a country woman whose head was tied up in a turban as wide as her shoulders. Another woman, who had a large pan of pineapples on her head, was carrying a baby on her back and dragging along a small-small boy wearing only a scanty shirt. The baby was laughing; the small boy was crying.

Everybody was busy. No one looked at Momolu or at those he followed. He wondered if they would stop to stare if they knew that he and Flumbo were going to stand before the commissioner to answer a serious charge, and that they might be imprisoned or in some other way punished and disgraced.

The threatening noise of a motorcar coming down the street sounded behind him. As it approached, people ran from the middle of the street. To Momolu, when he looked around, it was like seeing a huge shining beast with two great eyes and a yawning mouth howling its great sound. For a moment his legs seemed to have lost their power to move his body; then Jalla-Malla's strong arm pulled him away from the path of what

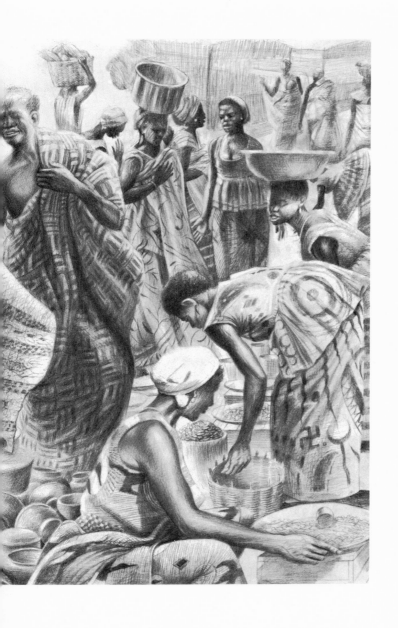

he was later to learn was called a bus. It was loaded with people who seemed wholly unafraid.

"It is magic!" he said, panting with excitement. "It is the greatest magic in the world!"

It was all too amazing for one fourteen-year-old boy fresh from the bush country. For himself it did not seem that his heart would ever lie down, that he could ever be at peace among these people who were civilized. He longed for the quiet of Lojay. His father's house was good. The life his people lived was the life all the people of the world should follow.

Here in Cape Roberts there were too many ways of living, of talking, of wearing clothes; there were too many things to fear in this thing of being civilized and this thing of government. "I fear! I fear!" he repeated softly to himself.

He remembered then something Chief Logomo had said, "A brave man faces danger."

One day in Lojay long ago the chief had commended Momolu for not running away from trouble. He had said that Momolu was a worthy son of Flumbo. That time Momolu had spoken out and said that the blame for mischief was to be placed on his head. So it was. So it should be again. The punishment must fall on him, not on his father.

True, Jalla-Malla would speak out in their behalf, and Jalla-Malla knew the government man called commissioner. Old Tinsoo too, bearing the staff of the chief, would speak with all the authority of Lojay. There would be enough to speak, but all their words might be of no avail. In Kewpessie country it was said, "Talk comes out of the mouth, but rice goes in."

Words in any speech, or even in every speech, would not fill a man's belly when he was hungry, and all the words of Jalla-Malla and Tinsoo and Flumbo and Momolu—all their words together would not replace the five bags of rice which now lay at the bottom of the river.

It would take something more. Some price would have to be paid, something worth as much as five bags of rice.

Momolu stopped. His head bowed forward; his hands went to his breast.

"I? Momolu?" His lips moved forming the words, but no sound came. For just a little time he stood; then his head went up, and he moved forward again. His steps had been short and uncertain before; now that he knew what he must do, his bare feet came down firm and strong on the clay road. He knew what he must do now; he was sure. He thought of Portee, his gentle mother, and of their pleasant three-roomed house with the open porch, but he put the thought from his mind. He must, he would, be the one to pay the price. He was surely worth as much as five bags of rice, and with himself he would make up the debt, and his father should go home a free man.

They were at the great white government house now. Momolu did not walk up the wide steps; he did not walk; he marched. A soldier pacing back and forth before the door looked at the boy from the bush country, and Momolu, seeing the look, thought that the soldier must be admiring his straight back and his high held head.

In the long high-ceilinged room the scene was not like that in a country palaver house. This was a Liberian military office; the floors were of wood, and the people in charge all wore soldiers' uniforms. The room did not stand open to the air except at the windows that let in sunshine which twinkled on the gold buttons of the officers and on the shiny metal objects lying on the table.

A fat Liberian officer with a smooth bald head was sitting at the table, smoking a cigar. At his side a thin young soldier was writing in a book. His face bore the marks of some African tribe. Using the American speech, Jalla-Malla spoke to the young man. The soldier turned over some papers with his hand, and finding the right one, he wrote on it as he called out something in American speech, pointing with his hand toward Flumbo and Momolu.

A soldier in plain uniform with a red cap on his head came forward then, and put iron bracelets on Flumbo's right wrist and Momolu's left. The two bracelets were linked together by a chain, and so Momolu found himself tied to his father as he had never before been tied. With a shove they were started toward the end of the room. The soldier followed them and with signs made them know that they should sit on the floor with others who were chained, two by two, in the same way.

These men were prisoners, and Momolu himself was a prisoner. He was a prisoner, and Flumbo his father, chained to him now, was a prisoner with him. A feeling of shame swept over him. His eyes closed; his head bowed. He started to lift his hands to cover his face, but only his right hand was free.

"Never mind, Momolu," Flumbo said beside him. "Never mind."

Shame! Momolu thought. Why should the soldiers chain them so? For five days of their own free will they had traveled to come to this place. Why would anyone think they would now try to run away? Run away in this strange town where they were foreigners? Perhaps they thought that he, Momolu, might try to escape, but they could not think that of his father. Surely anyone could tell that Flumbo was a man whose heart was both strong and good. They were father and son, and they were not rogues.

Flumbo was a man whose heart was both strong and good, but while they sat waiting Momolu could feel his father's body trembling beside him.

The thin young soldier writing in the book looked up and called out. Two prisoners got to their feet, the iron bracelets clinking as they stumbled forward.

True, the scene was not like a palaver house in the country, but the court palaver seemed much the same. One of the prisoners wore only a loincloth. The other stood in a pair of soiled white pants and a ragged shirt with faded blue stripes.

The thin young soldier lifted a brown bottle from the table and poured into the free hand of both the prisoners some thick white liquid. The prisoners lifted their hands to their mouths and licked their palms.

"Sassal juice," Flumbo whispered in Momulu's ear. "If he who tastes it does not tell the truth, he will die."

It was like the ceremony of the bush priests in Kewpessie country, but there the accused was forced to drink a cup of sap from a poison tree. Momulu had never known a man to die, because, he thought, none would drink and dare to lie. Some had become very sick, and it was said that though they had not lied, they had been mistaken in what they said.

A soldier with the marks of a sergeant on his sleeve spoke first. Then the prisoner with the striped shirt spoke in his own defense. The man in the loincloth said nothing. He stood motionless as though he did not understand or as though he did not care; he showed no sign of agreeing or disagreeing with what was said about him.

The fat Liberian officer asked some questions of the sergeant and of the striped-shirt prisoner. Then he spoke to the silent one. The man lifted his head, but he still said nothing. The captain shouted at him, but the prisoner only smiled. The captain picked up one of his books and looked at something in it. He spoke again and slapped his hand on the table. The prisoners were led away.

"Flumbo . . . Momolu . . . ." The writing soldier was reading something aloud from his paper. Momolu did not understand all the words, but he heard his name and the name of his father, and he knew that his time had come.

He wanted to act unafraid, but as he tried to stand, his legs buckled under him, and he would have staggered had not Flumbo's arm been steady at his side. Strength from Flumbo seemed to flow into him as they walked forward together to take their place before the table. Momolu stood erect and stretched himself to stand tall. Words were said; when the sassal juice was poured into his hand, he closed his eyes and took his portion on his tongue and licked his palm. It did not taste like poison. Perhaps, he thought, it only tastes like poison when a lie has been told.

Old Tinsoo stood close beside Flumbo. Beyond him Jalla-Malla leaned over the table, smiling at the bald-headed officer and talking softly. The officer did not return the smile, but he nodded his agreement.

The soldier with the papers read something aloud. Jalla-Malla turned and spoke to Flumbo. "The man says the government is vexed because you make war with soldiers in Lojay, that you caused the men of Lojay to hurt the soldiers and tear their clothes, and now the man says that you must speak the truth and say if it be so."

"It be so!" Flumbo agreed.

When Jalla-Malla had repeated Flumbo's answer, the fat officer sat up straight and talked.

Jalla-Malla turned again to Flumbo. "Now this man is the commissioner," he said. "He wants you to tell him why you did so. You must tell him just as you told me, and I will put your words in the American speech and he will understand."

As Flumbo told his story, Momolu wanted to join in. He wanted to explain that the sergeant was a fine fellow and that they were really only making play and that for true his father was a man of peace and did not start to fight the soldier, that

113

the sergeant was the one who attacked Flumbo first. This was what he wanted to explain, but the time was not yet his to speak.

Flumbo finished his story, "Now when I came with my son to bring the rice, just as the captain and my chief said I must, we met trouble on the river. Five bags of the rice we lose."

While the commissioner listened to the story from Jalla-Malla, he frowned. When he heard the end, he slapped his hand on the table and shouted at Flumbo.

Jalla-Malla started talking again. At first it seemed that he was angry too, and Momolu was surprised that he should talk so to a government man. Then it seemed that Jalla-Malla was begging. He smiled and tried to get the commissioner to be satisfied, but the fat officer turned himself sideways in his chair and took out a fresh cigar and lit it with a shiny gold fire-pot in his hand. The tangy smell of tobacco filled the room. The commissioner seemed hardly to listen as Jalla-Malla called on Tinsoo to say his part.

Tinsoo bowed low, and what he said came softly from his lips. He showed Chief Logomo's rod of authority and laid it on the table. The officer

114

took it up and examined it, especially the end which was made of gold.

Momolu knew that Tinsoo was saying that all the people of Lojay knew Flumbo was a man of courage and honesty and that the fight was a thing of misunderstanding and the loss of the rice was an accident and the lost rice would be replaced, but when he ended, the commissioner only shook his head and told the soldier what to write.

"I did all I could for you," Jalla-Malla said, putting his hands on the two handcuffed hands of Flumbo and Momolu. "The commissioner says that this palaver cannot be finally settled now. When the captain who was at Lojay comes again they will have the whole palaver again. Until that time you must wait in prison. There is nothing more for me to say. His heart is hard."

"Let me speak!" Momolu's voice was thin at first. He leaned forward and tried to speak his Kewpèssie words loudly and clearly as though by sounding them so the commissioner would understand.

"It is I, Momolu, who made all the trouble. You must know this, and when you know you will not make Flumbo, my father, go to prison.

"It was I, Momolu, who made play with the sergeant soldier, and it was I, Momolu, who made the canoe turn bottom over so that all five bags of rice were lost. Five bags of rice, only five bags of rice! And if my father goes to sit in prison, where then will five bags of rice again come from? But I am young and I am strong, and one who has me to work for him will find that I am worth more than five bags of rice.

"I beg you then, do not hold Flumbo, my father, but take me and let me work a year or five years or ten years to fulfill the payment for the five bags of rice. Take me and use my strong arms, but let him go, I beg you. Let him go back to Portee, my mother. Let him go back to his house and land. Let him go, and I will stay and make you better than five bags of rice."

Momolu was crying when he finished his speech, not crying as a child cries because he is angry, but tears were running down his cheeks and dropping on the table. His right arm was outstretched and he moved it toward Flumbo, toward the commissioner, and toward himself by turn. His left hand, bound to Flumbo's right, tugged at the irons that made them prisoner.

116

The commissioner watched him, and when Momolu stopped talking, he took his cigar from his mouth and told the younger officer what he should write. Then, in a gesture of dismissal, he waved his hand.

Tinsoo put his arm around Momolu's shaking shoulders as a sergeant led them from the room.

"The commissioner would not hear your brave words," he said. "He says the law is in the book. My heart is good for you."

12

Momolu was not prepared for the prison.

In Lojay there was a house in which people were sometimes confined. It was not much of a house, and most of the time Chief Logomo used it only for a storage place. Momolu with Dairku and other Lojay boys had peered into its darkness once when the door was open. Boxes and things that were no longer useful were piled there in disorder. A carved wooden mask and a shaggy monkey-skin coat hung on the wall. An old hammock with its broken frame leaned below it. Sometimes a stranger caught prowling like a rogue or a man who was crazed with evil spirits might be held there. It was a strong house with a heavy wooden door held fast with chains and a large flat lock opened only by a key which Chief Logomo carried on a leather thong about his waist.

The prison in Cape Roberts was dark but otherwise very different. For one thing it was dirtier than anything Momolu had ever expected to see. One long low-ceilinged room made of corrugated iron, it was also hot and dark. The air was so rancid from the smell of unwashed bodies and the accumulations of filth on the floor that Momolu tried to take as little of the air as possible into his lungs. At the ends of the building, narrow barred windows admitted only enough light to show an uneven row of dark shadows on each side. The other prisoners were handcuffed together in pairs like Momolu and his father, and their handcuffs were locked in turn to chains hanging down from beams in the ceiling.

No one spoke while the soldiers led Momolu and Flumbo in and locked them to the chain that held them to a small circle. The prisoners stared, blinking in the light that came through the open door. As soon as the soldiers left, voices were raised. Men shifted position, rattling their chains.

"I am Flumbo from Lojay town in Kewpessie

country," Flumbo called out. "Is there one here who speaks as a Kewpessie man?"

"Kewpessie! Kewpessie!" The word was repeated around the prison. Many voices repeated the word, but one, louder than the others, shouted out the name and laughed. Again and again the voice called out, "Kewpessie! Kewpessie!" and laughed harder and harder, until others joined in the laughter and some called out as though in anger.

"Kewpessie fool! Kewpessie fool!" The wild voice yelled.

Flumbo called again, "Kewpessie man! I hear you now."

"Kewpessie!" The other laughed again. "Sometimes I walk about I see Kewpessie country. I know and like Kewpessie words. I no like Kewpessie man. Kewpessie man be fool. Same way Gola man be fool. Same way Kru man be fool. Same way Bassa man be fool. Same way Liberian man be fool. Liberian man be fool past all." He laughed again long and loud, and some of the others laughed with him.

"Talk sense, man." Flumbo called out. "Talk sense!"

He strained at his chain, leaning forward, trying to see through the darkness the one who spoke the words of the Kewpessie tribe, who spoke Kewpessie words and laughed senselessly. Others started talking again. Some nearby were shouting at Flumbo, but their words were strange to him. Of all those in prison none it seemed could speak to him save that one who laughed and yelled out nonsense words and laughed again.

"The witches have taken that one's mind," Flumbo said. "He is crazy."

Crazy? Momolu knew what it was to be crazy. There was a woman in Lojay who at certain times would laugh and cry by turn and tear her clothes from her body and pull her hair from her head, and those who loved her would then bind her so that she might not harm herself. The witches had taken her mind, and she was crazy.

This man, then, was like that, and there was no other man there in prison to tell the father and son from Kewpessie country what their life might be or what they might do to ease the hardships. There was no one to tell them what the soldiers might order them to do or to speak to the guards for them about their needs.

How long must they wait in prison? Would it be until Nisa-Way went back to Lojay and returned with five more bags of rice to pay the fine? How long would it be before the captain and his soldiers came again? How long would it be before they held the next palaver? How long? How long?

Even as his gaze wandered about the place seeking for answers, Momolu knew none could be found. His eyes became accustomed to the gloom; he looked into his father's face.

"Never mind, Momo," Flumbo said. "Sun sleeps, but time goes on, and the sun comes back again."

But it seemed to Momolu that the sun could never again shine as it had in Lojay now that he was a prisoner here with his father, chained like some wild thing in this foul place. He was a prisoner. All his friends at home would know if ever he returned that he had been a prisoner. They would not treat him as an equal. Dairku and Billidee and all the others would not want him as their friend. His father's friends would turn their backs at Flumbo's approach, and they would no longer listen to his words in the palaver house.

When Momolu thought of his father's disgrace, he could not bear it. A lump rose in his throat, choking him. He began to cry. He cried as a baby cries, and he could not control himself.

Flumbo, chained to him by his right hand, twisted his body to reach over with his left hand and hold Momolu's shoulder.

"Momolu! Stop it!" he said sharply. "Are you a small boy crying for his mama? All this time you have stood as a man. You spoke as a man to the commissioner. Must you be a baby now?"

"O Pa, my father! My father! My heart turns over. I fear!"

"What is there to fear now?" Flumbo pushed his son's head up so that he could look into Momolu's face. "Tell me, what do you fear now? You had cause to fear before you saw this place. Now you have seen. Now you know what it is. Now you have only to wait, and tomorrow will be like today, and the day after will be just the same; then one day it will be over, and we will wash our skins in clean water with strong soap and go again to Lojay, to our own house. The sun will shine and warm our backs. The good things from your mother's pots will fill our bellies, and those who love us will hold us tighter than these chains."

"But our friends, Pa!" Momolu was comforted, but he could not forget the disgrace. "Our friends will know that we have been prisoners, and they will despise us."

"When a man is sick with fever, is he not a prisoner in his own house? Or if a man's leg is torn by alligators, is he not chained? A man's friends will keep. They will keep and wait and do for him when he cannot do for himself."

"Nisa-Way is your friend." Even as he said it, Momolu felt better. Nisa-Way would never turn his back on Flumbo. Even now he was probably paddling back to Lojay with all his strength to replace the five bags that had been lost. "Nisa-Way is your friend, and Tinsoo too!"

"Yes," Flumbo answered, "Nisa-Way is more than a friend. He is a brother, and so are Tinsoo and Jalla-Malla. A man has many brothers if his heart is right."

Momolu had not noticed in his distress that the other prisoners had been making more noise. They were rattling their chains and beating drum-fashion on cans, calling from side to side and up and down the lines. As his father spoke he had to shout to make himself heard. The pair of men handcuffed together next to Momolu seemed to be angry with each other. One was old and thin; the other looked younger, but he too was so thin his long hand was like the claw of a big bird. He moved it in the air, close to the old man's nose, as though he were going to strike his mate, or worse, seize him and tear him to pieces.

While Momolu watched and wondered what they were saying, forgetting his own troubles for the time, the noise of shouting and beating on cans and the rattling of chains suddenly stilled. Turning like the others toward the other end of the room, he saw the small door open. A soldier stepped inside, bending low to get through the door.

"Food," Flumbo said behind him.

All around the other prisoners were calling out. Two men in ragged clothes came crouching through the door behind the soldier. They carried large white pans, and starting at the ends of the two lines nearest the door, they stopped before each pair of men.

The prisoners in their turn reached into the pan as it passed, each man dipping in with his cupped hands and taking out a portion of rice. Each was allowed to take out as much rice as his two hands could hold. Fastened as they were with one man's right hand chained to his mate's left, some were awkward, but others moved as if by long practice, coming up with great mounds of rice without spilling anything.

Before the pan reached Momolu and Flumbo, it was empty; the man who carried it had to go back to the door for more.

The sight of the men eating like animals and the awful smell of filth made Momolu's stomach lose its desire for food. When the pan finally came before him, he started to pull back, but Flumbo said, "We must eat!"

Flumbo cupped his hands together, and Momolu, following his father's example, dipped with him. Some of the rice fell through his fingers to the ground, and as he bent his head into his hands to eat he lost still more. The rice was well cooked; bits of fish were boiled with it. It was seasoned with salt and pepper, and moist with palm oil. In any other place he would have eaten heartily and called it good. In prison it took on the evil of the place. He ate little.

While the soldier and the men who carried the pans were in the prison, there was little talking. When they were gone and the door closed, the prisoners raised their voices again, but now that they had eaten it seemed there was less anger. Some had eaten as much as they would have had in their own homes. They might still quarrel among themselves, but now they were not hungry.

In Lojay all the people slept after their midday meal. In the prison at Cape Roberts the men also prepared to sleep. The skinny man chained to the old one called to Flumbo and pointed with his foot to a can on the floor. Momolu had not thought about it, but now he knew that the only way the prisoners could relieve themselves was by such means.

From the beam overhead the tall thin man pulled down a piece of sacking and a ragged blanket. With the blanket wrapped about him, he sat on the floor with his back against the back of the old man who covered himself as well as he could with the dirty bag.

Others along the line, some with blankets of one kind or another, were settling down to sleep.

Momolu and Flumbo had nothing for their comfort. To sit in the filth on the floor was unthinkable.

"My pants," Momolu said, "I will not sleep and let my good pants be in the dirt."

"Your pants or your skin?" Flumbo smiled for the first time. "Today we can stand or rest somehow without sitting or lying on the ground." Flumbo crouched into a half-sitting position, drawing Momolu downward so that their bodies leaned one against the other. "So we can do for now, but if we stay here long we will have to do like the others."

Momolu's heart jumped. Pa had said, "If we stay here long." Why did he speak so? It had taken five days to make the trip from Lojay paddling with the current. Surely it would take Nisa-Way many more days to go and come again, and they would surely have to stay as many nights.

But Flumbo had smiled and then he had said, "If we stay here long."

"How many days do you count that we must stay?" Momolu asked.

"A man has brothers." Momolu could feel the shrug of Flumbo's shoulders. "A man has brothers whose hands are not tied. Our brothers will count the time for us."

Whether the days and the nights would be few or many, Momolu thought he would never be able to sleep in this place. When exhaustion overcame him, he planned to take off his pants and fold them to make a pad on which to sit. Once they had been on the ground, he would not wear them again. During the daytime while he stood, the pants could rest on the beam overhead. Flumbo with his robe could probably do the same.

Brothers whose hands were not tied would count the days . . . Surely these others whose thin bodies were covered with open sores, these others might have brothers too, but the days they counted were many.

One day Flumbo and Momolu would wash their skin clean once again, and the bright sun would warm them and those they loved would hold them tight. Portee would hold Momolu again as when he was a small boy and his heart would lie down.

Momolu fell asleep. In the quiet gloom of Cape Roberts' prison he slept and dreamed of his mother in Lojay. A shudder passed over his frame.

Flumbo twisted about, and with his free arm held his son so that Momolu's proud pants should not rest on the ground.

Along the double line of dark crouching forms, men talked softly among themselves, and some muttered or cried out in their troubled sleep. The crazy man who knew the Kewpessie speech was singing and tapping with his fingers on a can.

In Momolu's dream the sunlight fell like tiny drops of rain and warmed his back and glittered on the trees and grass and housetops. Bama's drum was calling, calling all the people of the Kewpessie country, and in Lojay a sea of faces stretched from the waterside to the wall of forest; houses stood up like islands, and all the people were smiling and happy with their faces turned up to the sun, and Flumbo was answering Bama's call: "I hear your word! I hear your word!"

Momolu's eyes opened. It was Flumbo's voice, but it was the gloom of evening—then he remembered. Around him were angry voices as unhappy men awakened from their dreams.

Among the voices, one voice called in the speech Momolu knew, "Kewpessie man stand up!

Your brothers come for you now! Stand up! Stand up and meet your brothers!"

Again Flumbo answered, "I hear your word."

He was helping Momolu get to his feet as the small door opened and a soldier came in. He walked straight down the line and stopped by Flumbo and Momolu. With a key he unlocked the chain fastening them to the ceiling beam and motioned them toward the open door.

It was only a small door, but in the shadow of the long dark room, it seemed to shine of itself. Momolu hurried toward it, stepping with the rhythm of the song the crazy man had started to sing as he drummed with his fingers on a can:

> Kewpessie brothers be strong-O.
> Kewpessie brothers be strong-O.
> Kewpessie brothers be strong-O.
> Strong brothers break the iron chain.

Flumbo laid his free hand on the shoulder of the singer as he passed, and at the door when Momolu would have rushed out into the bright sunlight, Flumbo stopped and turned. As Flumbo raised his right hand, Momolu's left hand went up with it. Together they waved, and before them it seemed a sea of faces stretched from one dark wall to the other; and hands were waving and voices were calling out different words that said farewell; and all the faces turned toward the little light that passed through the door and none of the faces were happy.

13

Momolu remembered that Flumbo had not lost heart in prison. His father had said that he counted on the help of brothers, but Momolu had thought only of Nisa-Way and old Tinsoo who would have to journey all the way back to Lojay.

Jalla-Malla had proven to be a brother close at hand. He had bought five bags of rice in the market, and with ten bags carried on the heads of as many men, he had returned to the commissioner. His soft words made the officer smile, and it was agreed that Flumbo and his son could leave the prison if Jalla-Malla would guard them until they should be called.

It was good to smell fresh air again. It was not like the sweet country air of Lojay, but after the prison, Momolu was happy to fill and refill his lungs. The smell of prison clung to him until he shed his clothes and washed with spring water and strong soap and splashed in the salt sea water. Then he knew he was clean again.

As Momolu thought about it, he remembered that he had not heard anyone talking the American way in prison. He wondered how it would have been if he had been able to talk to the commissioner in the commissioner's own tongue . . . and if he had understood the magic of the book. Perhaps the soldier writing in the book at the table with the commissioner had learned the book's magic at some mission. Birmah might some day be sitting at a table writing the things of government. And John, son of Jalla-Malla, was only a small boy, but he had learned.

"Some day," he told himself, "I, Momolu, will know the magic of the book."

On the morning after their release, Momolu and Flumbo were fishing with Jalla-Malla and others of Kru Town. They stood knee-deep in the water, working with casting nets that were round and measured from side to side about two lengths of the body. The net was thrown with a wide,

sweeping motion. The weighted edges sank, but the center was held up by a line from the fisherman's hand. The fish would be trapped under this middle part.

Across the river a plane was moving slowly on the water. Flumbo and Momolu and those with them stopped their work to watch. A steady roar came from the great machine. People along the shore were waving. For the first time Momolu saw how huge a plane could be. He still believed that it was only by power of magic that it was able to fly.

The plane moved away—upstream—still gliding on the water, and then it turned and with a greater roar swiftly came again raising itself out of the water into the air. Momolu and those with him shouted their delight when they saw the sight. They watched and pointed as the plane moved higher and higher, farther and farther away. After a time, the plane became no larger than a bird.

It had taken people away from Cape Roberts. The lands they would visit! A machine that was able to fly like a bird with many people in its belly! It could be that those who had gone would never return. They might never again have to look on the face of a Liberian commissioner. They might never see the inside of a Liberian prison. They would be free.

"Pa," Momolu said to his father, "now I see what we must do."

Flumbo was bending over his net and Momolu joined him. With their hands they were taking the fat-bodied red snappers they had caught and stringing them on a leather line tied to a stake.

When the net was cleared, Flumbo lifted it up and turned. "So! My son looks at a machine that flies away, and he sees what he must do."

Momolu spoke again. "It can be if we go on a plane the plane will carry us to a far country." He was watching Flumbo's face. "If we go away from Liberian country and never come again, the commissioner cannot follow, and by and by he can forget."

Flumbo took a step away from his son. He swung his net in a wide circle and cast it far from him. It opened like a great flower and settled gently on the water, its edges sinking first, its center belling upward. Flumbo had thrown it like one who has always fished with such a net.

"My son's words are true," he said. "If we go far away and in our country no man sees the faces of Flumbo and Momolu, the commissioner can forget. By and by our people in Lojay can forget and never speak our names again.

"But what of you yourself? Could Momolu forget?" Flumbo asked, and splashed away to see what might have been caught inside his net.

They had started fishing in the first gray light of day. As the sun rose higher in the sky and looked down into the water, the snappers and whiteys and striped tiger fish moved out into deeper waters. Those who fished gathered up their nets, and Jalla-Malla let Momolu carry on his head their basket of fish as they made their way to market.

There Jalla-Malla gave all their fish to one of the market women to sell. She made some markings in a book while she talked with Jalla-Malla, who seemed to be telling her about Flumbo and Momolu.

"Mama Zomah says," Jalla-Malla told them, "that if every day you will bring your share of fish to her, she will make a mark in her book, and on big market day, which we call Saturday, she will give you the money for them."

It was still early morning when Momolu and the others returned to Kru Town, but John had already gone up the hill to the mission. Momolu was eager to go again to see his "brother" Birmah, and since there was no work for him to do, Flumbo agreed. On Sunday when he first found his Kewpessie friend at the mission, Birmah had seemed happy to greet him. When they parted, it had been agreed that Momolu should visit again.

This time it was different. The buildings no longer seemed so shiny white or as large as they had seemed before. Arriving on the hill, Momolu asked for Birmah, forgetting that his friend now used another name, but someone remembered who he was and Birmah was brought to see him.

On Sunday Birmah had been wearing fresh white clothes. On this day he wore faded blue pants and a shirt that was not very clean. Birmah did not say he was glad to see Momolu, and the way he acted and spoke made Momolu wish he had never come.

The missionary man saw them talking together. He called something to Birmah, but he did not speak to Momolu. Birmah was saying that he must go to do some work when the woman missionary came out of the house. She smiled when she saw Birmah with Momolu and said something, calling Birmah by his American name, David.

Birmah dropped his head as though in shame. "Mission mommy says you must come and eat with us," he told Momolu.

Momolu did not want to go. He did not think that Birmah wanted to take him to join the mission boys who were going into the long open shed where the tables were. He would rather have turned and made his way back down the hill, but the white woman was standing waiting. She beckoned for Momolu to follow Birmah.

The woman led the two boys to one of the long tables around which the mission boys were standing. She spoke to them, and they moved so that there was room for Momolu to stand beside Birmah with the others.

While they stood quietly, someone started singing. It was a sweet song. It made Momolu a little sad, but it was sweet to his ears. When the song was over, they sat and ate.

Momolu was not comfortable. He started to use his fingers to pick up the food, but Birmah nudged him, and when he turned, Birmah told him to eat like the others. For each boy there were spoons and forks which were smaller than those the Kewpessie people used in cooking. Here the boys used them to put food into their mouths. Momolu tried but ate only a little.

Trying not to stare, he looked from one to the other of the boys. On Sunday all of them had seemed friendly and good and very wise. Now they were laughing at him, and they were not friendly. They looked neither good nor wise.

Momolu had no stomach for the food. As soon as he had eaten enough to be polite, he told Birmah that he must leave. Stopping in front of the woman missionary, he bowed and said in Kewpessie, "You have a good heart for Momolu who comes from Lojay."

As he hurried down the rocky pathway toward Kru Town, he remembered her smile and his heart lay down.

The days passed swiftly. Early each morning before the sun got up, his father awakened Momolu, and together they went out to fish. In the late afternoon they fished again. After the morning's work Momolu would walk about in the town.

He liked best to go with Jalla-Malla who knew many people and could answer all his questions.

He learned that the people on the low coastal plain lived their lives in different ways. Most of the African people were of the Kru tribe but many of the Gola and Bassa and some of the Kewpessie lived among them. From down the coast had come the Ashantis and Fantees, and from the north, the Vays and Mandingoes. The Krus had their own laws handed down from father to son, and in each town a chief governed with the aid of a council of old men.

Also on the coast lived the Liberians, the grandchildren and great-grandchildren of Africans who in olden times had been taken to far America as slaves. Some of the Liberians had dark skins, but some of them were not very dark. They lived in the American way in large houses of wood and stone and corrugated iron, but they called themselves brothers to the Africans. They were the people of government, and their laws were higher than those of the African tribes. Their power stretched over all the land, up and down the coast, and far back up the rivers into the bush. Their children were taught by wise men and women, so that they understood many things that were mysteries to the simple people of the African countryside.

Then there were the white people, some from America and others from lands called England and Holland and Germany and France. The white people were few in number, but they were very important. A few were missionaries, but most of them were in trade. Their ships, greater than any man-made thing Momolu had ever seen, brought their people and their goods to Africa and took away palm oil and palm nuts and logs of hard gumwood and other things that African people had to trade.

One day as Momolu was walking with Jalla-Malla along the street of open-front shops, Jalla-Malla stopped to talk with a man leaning against a truck. Standing still, the truck seemed to hold no danger, and Momolu considered it. In the flat, boxlike part of the body, enough rice could be carried to feed a family for the space of a year. Momolu felt it and looked carefully to see its different parts, the wheels under it, the seats, the shiny glass parts like eyes.

To amuse Momolu, Jalla-Malla's friend showed

him how the lights could be turned on and off.

"The voice?" Momolu asked. "How does it know when to make a roar?"

Jalla-Malla repeated this to his friend in his own speech. The man reached inside, and the wild noise, like no animal Momolu had ever heard, came forth again from the front. They laughed, the men, at the country boy's fright, but once Momolu saw the place to touch, he pressed his own hand there again and again, and then he lost his fear.

"Would you like to ride?" Jalla-Malla asked. "Our friend will take us in his truck."

When they had seated themselves inside the part that was like a small house with Momolu between the two men, he tried his best to see what the friend would do. He wanted to remember so he could tell the boys in Lojay.

The driver touched some things with his hands and some other things with his feet. The truck seemed suddenly to be a live thing wakened from sleep. It was made, Momolu knew, of iron and wood, but under him, the soft seat trembled like an excited animal.

Momolu wanted to get out, but the truck had

begun to move. The awful noise sounded. People jumped from the truck's path. The driver turned his wheel first to one side and then to the other. At the end of the street where the government house stood, the truck turned and started up a hill. Momolu had never seen this part of Cape Roberts.

Few people were in the road. The houses were large, and they stood far apart. The truck was moving swiftly and smoothly. Momolu had never traveled so fast. The seat under him bounced, but the feeling was not as though the thing were angry. Riding was good, and Momolu was no longer afraid.

Over the hill and down again, and along a level stretch of road they rolled, moving faster and faster. Then it seemed that the truck was not moving but that all the world was flying past them, trees and shrubs and houses slipping along with the land. Ahead the scene would move toward them at first slowly, then faster, and suddenly it whizzed by. How would he ever be able to make Dairku understand it? There were no words to tell about it. The truck slowed as it climbed a long, steep hill. When they came over the crest, Momolu saw stretching below and far beyond the land the wide sweep of unending, sparkling sea.

The truck shook off the struggle of the climb, and lowering its nose, it rushed faster and faster with each moment, rushing toward the sea with those inside. The truck seemed angry now and anxious to destroy the men it bore. It was taking them out to drown them in the water. It was going too fast ever to stop.

Momolu looked sideways at the driver. He was crouched over with his hands holding fast to the wheel. His jaw was set in a hard line. His teeth were clenched. It was as if he too were holding on in terror.

"Stop! Stop!" Momolu shouted. "We will die in the water!"

Jalla-Malla laughed. Momolu tried to climb over him to get out, but Jalla-Malla held onto him. Momolu turned to get out the other side, but the driver's hands still clutched the wheel, and he was laughing too.

"Crazy!" Momolu shouted. "Now these men are crazy! Pa, come and save me! Mommy! They are crazy! Now I die! Now I die! O my little Mommy!"

He covered his face to shut out the sight of death and sobbed into his hands.

The movement slowed. The truck stopped. Jalla-Malla put his arm around Momolu's heaving shoulders. "Never mind, Momolu boy! Never mind!" he said.

Momolu lay back, his eyes closed, his breath coming in short gasps. "Sick," he finally muttered. It was the one word that he could utter.

Jalla-Malla stepped out and helped Momolu to follow. It was none too soon. Momolu vomited.

Sometime later he sat beside the road and looked at the truck. It had stopped far short of the water. The man, Jalla-Malla's friend, had stopped it. The truck was a thing that the driver had made a slave. He could make the truck work for him. He could make it carry himself and his friends, and in the back the truck could carry more bags of rice than many canoes could.

Momolu was still afraid of the truck, but Jalla-Malla and his friend were standing by it, leaning against it as they talked. The driver was the master. He was not afraid because he understood.

Momolu had never been more afraid, not even when he was in prison. Flumbo had said that in prison he should no longer fear because he knew. Flumbo was right. The man who had mastered the truck was not afraid because he understood.

"I, Momolu, will understand," he said softly, speaking only to himself. "I will understand these mysteries some day, and I will have no fear."

"Come," Jalla-Malla called, "we must go home now."

Momolu would rather have walked. Although he had said he would have no fear he knew he still did not understand, and so his legs became so weak that Jalla-Malla had almost to lift him to get him back into the seat.

He watched again the movements of the driver. The man's two hands and both his feet moved together. It was too much for one pair of eyes to know everything that was done, but as the truck was backed and turned and headed up the hill again, one thing seemed clear. When the driver wanted the machine to move toward the right, he turned the wheel in that direction. When it was to go straight ahead, he held the wheel still. This much Momolu could see. This much he learned.

"If I learn one thing today," he told himself, "I can learn something else another time. Then by and by I will understand and I will have no fear."

14

Momolu could not have counted the many things he learned each day at Cape Roberts. He kept his eyes open, and he listened whenever there was talk in words he understood.

Some things he did not like.

He heard talk of stealing. In Lojay every house was open. People did not take things that belonged to others. Here they had always to be on guard. The doors on the houses were fastened with locks. When clothes were washed and laid out to dry, the owner had to keep close watch over them. One day when Momolu stopped to rest with his load of fish, a man passing by snatched a big whitefish from Momolu's basket and ran off with it. Those who saw the wicked deed only laughed.

People seemed less friendly than they were in

the country. Even the men who had come from Kewpessie country were not friendly. They avoided the visitors, and if they had business with Jalla-Malla, they spoke in Kru or in the American tongue. Jalla-Malla said that they were busy, but old Tinsoo said that they were men of little heart. He told the story of the foolish vulture who found a dead parrot and who then picked his own feathers out and tried to cover himself with the bright feathers of the dead bird.

Momolu did not go again to the mission on the hill. When Sunday came, he watched Jalla-Malla and his family climb the hill without him. The next Sunday only John went, and when he came again, he made them know that the missionary had asked about them.

John did show Momolu his books, and he tried to explain his writing, but since they could not talk together, Momolu could only learn that the book palaver was not easy to understand.

On the day after the third Sunday word came that Flumbo and his son should go back to stand before the commissioner. At the government house they were again handcuffed together and told to sit with the other prisoners. They watched while others were being tried. The Liberian commissioner was the head man in every palaver, but it was clear that the man with the tribal marks on his face had an important part. He read from the papers, and he wrote as the commissioner commanded him. He was busy with papers and books, reading from them, writing in them.

Their turn came at last. The writing soldier called out. "Flumbo . . . Momolu!"

This time as he walked forward with Flumbo, Momolu's legs were steady under him. Tinsoo and Jalla-Malla joined them at the table, while the writing soldier read the message from the paper in his hand to the commissioner.

Momolu was looking at the small metal piece on the desk from which the commissioner had gotten fire to light his cigar. It was a man-made thing of gold, a slave for the man who knew how to use it. No fire could be seen. It seemed asleep, as the truck had been asleep before the driver woke it up and made it move. The first time he had thought the firebox was magic. Now he knew it was not magic but understanding.

The commissioner looked up. His eyes fell on

Momolu, and he smiled. As he talked with Jalla-Malla there was no anger in his voice. Then Jalla-Malla turned to Flumbo. "Commissioner says we wait for Captain Johnson himself. Soon he will come," he said. "He is the captain who was at Lojay."

Soon he did come. Jalla-Malla had hardly spoken when Momolu heard behind him the hard ring of boots on the wooden floor. At Lojay the captain had seemed to be very serious. When he approached the table, he laughed and shook hands with the commissioner. Then he spoke to Momolu and Flumbo and old Tinsoo, and it was as though he were truly glad to see them. Pointing to the handcuffs, he shook his head, and after some more talk a soldier came with a key and unfastened them.

The captain seated himself and talked to Tinsoo; presently the old man turned to Flumbo. "The heart of the captain man is very good for us," Tinsoo said. "He says he is glad that we have come with the rice, and now he knows that the people of Lojay are honorable and that the fight palaver was the head's mistake and not the heart's."

The captain spoke again, and Tinsoo said, "The man wants to know if Flumbo hates the soldiers now and fears to have his son know them."

"Say to the captain," Flumbo replied, "that my heart lies down. I know now that the captain is a just man. But," he added, "my heart cannot love soldiers."

"This we must not say." Tinsoo's voice was high. Momolu could not understand why his father added words which would make the captain angry.

"This we must say," Flumbo replied, raising his hands above his head.

Tinsoo stood silently, looking from Flumbo to the captain who waited to know what was said. When Tinsoo told him, he leaned over to talk with the commissioner.

Then it was the commissioner's turn to speak. His voice was hard, and Momolu thought that surely he was saying that Flumbo must go to prison again. Tinsoo's head fell forward. A look of sadness came over his face. The captain was nodding his agreement to the commissioner's words.

Tinsoo turned to Flumbo. "The commissioner says that you have had your chance to return to your home in peace. He says the government wants only peace in every part of the nation and trouble rises quickly when country people hate the soldiers who walk in peace to do their duty. Now he says he cannot let you go back to your house. He says that Flumbo with Momolu are to be prisoners of the captain."

The captain called for his sergeant. It was the same man who had been at Flumbo's house in Lojay. He saluted the captain and stood straight while orders were given him. Then he led Momolu and Flumbo from the room. On the wide steps of the government house, he stopped so that they could talk with their friends.

Old Tinsoo was more upset than anyone else. He scolded in his high voice, saying that Flumbo had spoken as a foolish man letting everyone know the thoughts in his heart. Now he, Tinsoo, Chief Logomo's messenger, would have shame on his head when he returned to Lojay. When he stood before the council, they would say that he had failed.

Flumbo did not seem to care. "A father must speak the truth," he said, "or his son will become a liar. What I have said, I have said. You must tell

the people of Lojay that if ever Flumbo comes
again to his house in Lojay he will be just the
same."

After Nisa-Way said good-bye to them and Jalla-
Malla promised to visit them in the place they
called the barracks where Flumbo and Momolu
were to be held, the sergeant led his prisoners
away.

Momolu was not afraid. In his heart he was
proud of his father. He had stood bravely, telling
the truth and facing danger. They were prisoners
again, but they were no longer chained, and they
were out in the open sunshine. Momolu did not
know what the barracks might be, but surely it
would not be worse than prison.

The sergeant led the way. Flumbo followed,
and Momolu came last. As they walked along the
same road that Momolu had ridden in the truck, a
car overtook them with its horn sounding need-
lessly, for they were already far over on one side
of the road. Momolu thought of the man who was
driving, pressing a certain place to make the horn
sound out, turning the wheel to right and to left as
he wanted the car to go. The driver was master

because he understood. Perhaps the commissioner was right. If the people of the country hated the government's soldiers, trouble would arise. For himself he did not share Flumbo's hatred of the soldiers, but he knew that he would always stand with his father. One thing he was glad to remember, Flumbo had said that the captain was just. Certainly if a man was just, it would not be easy to hate him.

They came over the last long hill where the road led down to the shiny blue of the sea. On his other trip in the truck Momolu had been too frightened and too sick to notice anything about him. Now he could see the smoothness of the road's hard-packed clay and the way trees and shrubs had been cut cleanly away on both sides. Toward the left the ground was low. Beyond the trees in that direction were the beach and the wide stretch of blue water. On the right the land sloped upward and on the crest of the hill there were some long low buildings painted green.

The sergeant pointed to the hilltop. "Barracks," he said.

A narrow side road led them up the hill. At the

top of the hill the road fanned out to right and left to circle the barracks area. Three long buildings faced the open square where a company of soldiers were marching forward and back, turning and reversing at their leader's call.

"Drill," the sergeant said, as they stopped to watch the marching soldiers. It was a word Momolu was to hear often while he was there. He had learned many new words in Cape Roberts. He would learn more at the barracks.

"Drill," Momolu repeated.

The sergeant smiled. "Flag," he said, pointing upward to where the flag of Liberia floated high from the top of the pole in the center of the square. A steady breeze from the sea was keeping it open wide with its red and white bars and its large white star in a field of blue.

The sergeant pushed his round red cap forward on his head and threw his shoulders back as he started across the drill field. On the long walk from town he had been at ease like other men. Now his step was quick, his knees stiff, and his arms swung smartly with each step. In this place he was a soldier and a leader of men.

Flumbo, limping on his bad leg, could not keep up with him, and Momolu would not, because it would not be right to pass his father.

Entering the screened door of a building, the sergeant made Flumbo know that he and Momolu should wait outside. Momolu smiled at his father. "It is not like the prison," he said.

"No," Flumbo admitted. "It looks like a place of peace, but you must not forget that soldiers are used for war. They are at peace only when all obey and none oppose them. I will not love them if I stay one year or forty."

The sergeant returned, followed by a younger man.

"I am Poobak," the younger soldier said as he bowed low. "I am a Kewpessie brother whose home is in Jawley. Now the sergeant tells me that you, Flumbo, and you, Momolu, are from Kewpessie country and that you are to be our visitors."

Momolu was happy to meet a soldier who was of the Kewpessie people, but Flumbo was not content.

"For true," he said as he put out his hand to

161

clasp the hand of the soldier who called himself a brother. "For true, Flumbo and Momolu, his son, from Lojay are glad to hold the hand of Poobak from Jawley, but in one thing our Kewpessie brother is mistaken. We are not visitors but prisoners, and though you are my brother, you are a soldier and all soldiers are enemies of country people. So it is."

Poobak said Flumbo and Momolu would have to work, but he would help them as much as he could. Flumbo did not argue with the soldier, but it was clear that he was not willing to accept favors. He said that he would do what he was told, as every prisoner should, but in his heart he would not change. Momolu said nothing. Poobak took them through the camp. The building where they had met was called headquarters. There were many officers there, and rooms filled with supplies—tools, food, clothing, guns, and boxes of cartridges which made the guns shoot. One end of the building was where the captains and other officers who were called lieutenants and the chief officer who was called major slept.

The other two buildings were for soldiers. Each man had his own place on the floor to spread his sleeping mat and his place on the wall to hang his gun. On the far side of the hill, sloping toward the valley, was a village of native houses for the soldiers who had wives. While they were in Cape Roberts, they lived with their families much the same as other men lived.

Poobak had his house there, and a Bassa woman for his wife. She was only a young girl, scarcely as old as Momolu's sister, Sindah. They had no children. Flumbo and Momolu would eat at Poobak's house each day, but they were given mats and clean blankets and a place to sleep in the barracks.

For the rest of this first day Momolu was excited by what he saw. He listened carefully to everything Poobak said. That night as he wrapped his blanket about him and lay down to sleep, he tried to remember the new words, saying them softly to himself: "Barracks—officer—headquarters—forward march—halt—lieutenant—ammunition—"

He knew he was not saying some of the words right, but he would learn, and he would understand.

He was almost asleep when he heard the blow

ing of the horn; "bugle" was the soldier's word for it, he thought. Its song was loud, and yet it seemed soft. It was like a soldier's sharp command, and yet in some way he could not explain, it was sad also. Around him soldiers were saying their last good nights, and then all was quiet.

15

The song of the bugle, the last thing Momolu heard at night, was the first thing he heard in the morning. The morning bugle was not sad. It was sharp and fast, rousing all who heard it more quickly than the pepper bird at home.

Momolu jumped up and threw his blanket from him. Wearing only his loincloth, he ran out, not waiting for Flumbo, to go down the hill to wash himself in the stream of fresh cool water where the soldiers bathed. They spoke to him and smiled. He would have answered their greetings in his own speech, saying "Day comes now!" but most of the soldiers said, "Good morning," and he remembered that it was the American speech, so he said, "Good morning," too, and all about him there was laughter.

165

Up on the hill the bugle sounded again, and the soldiers hurried with their washing. Momolu was slower than the men. He was not used to so much hurry.

When he got back up the hill, the soldiers were lined up on the parade ground, and orders were being called. He wanted to get dressed and return to watch so he ran into the building where Flumbo had already rolled up his own mat and Momolu's. He was sweeping the floor.

"Good morning, Pa!" Momolu called proudly, using the American speech.

Flumbo stopped sweeping. He turned, and there was no answering smile on his face. "Now," he said slowly, "I see I am losing my son. The soldiers are stealing his heart. They call you with American words." He raised the broom as he moved toward Momolu. "They call you, and you want to answer, but I will not let you go from me."

With his left hand he seized Momolu's shoulder and spun him around and brought the broom handle down hard on Momolu's back. Again and again he struck.

"You are a boy of Lojay! You are not a soldier!

You will be Kewpessie and not American. You are my son. I will not let you go. Kewpessie! Do you hear? Kewpessie! Kewpessie! Kewpessie!"

Everything was twisted and broken in Momolu's thoughts. This was his father who was beating him. Flumbo's words were harder than the broomstick. When it was over, he lay on the floor. His back hurt, but it was not the physical pain that made him sob. He had been beaten before, but every other time it had been for a reason that he understood. The last time had been more than a year ago after he had neglected his work and then argued with Portee, his mother. Now he was nearly fifteen years old, and he had been beaten for having used American words to his father. For true, he was Kewpessie. No one would deny it. But must a Kewpessie, man or boy, always follow only the things of country people?

Around him soldiers came and walked about, but no one spoke to him. Outside the bugle sounded again. Whistles were being blown and orders given. He did not know how long he lay there. It was hot. He was thirsty and hungry. His back still hurt, and he was all mixed up in his thoughts. He heard footsteps approach, and then he felt the hand of his father gently rubbing his bruised back with a pungent ointment that at first stung and then soothed him.

When he raised himself and turned to look at his father, Flumbo's face was grave. He was sad, and in his eyes was a look of worry, such as Momolu had seldom seen.

He said, speaking softly, "I bring water. Drink."

Momolu sat up and took the gourd bowl in his two hands. The water was good.

Flumbo was peeling a boiled cassava. The long root looked like a sweet potato, but inside the rough skin the meat was white. Momolu ate it gladly.

"When the right hand works against the left," Flumbo said, "the heart sees trouble. So it is in my house. My son has stood with me in my trouble, and we have been prisoners together side by side. Now my son goes from me, and when I should be strong, I become weak. When my heart says I must draw my son, my hand drives him away. Momo, hear my word; I am sorry."

Momolu did not know what to say. Flumbo had done no wrong. He, Momolu, had been foolish to be so playful while they were still prisoners of the soldiers. He wanted to speak, but the words would not come. He wanted to say that they were yet together, father and son, and nothing could come between them to make him leave his father's side.

"My work is finished," Flumbo said. "I go to walk about. You will come with me?"

Momolu nodded and got up. He put on his pants and shirt. He followed his father out of the barracks and down the hill at the back. As they passed by the village of country houses, those who saw them only looked at them. They neither smiled nor spoke in greeting.

When they reached the beach of clean white sand, they stood for a while just looking at the broad shining water.

Then Flumbo drew his robe over his head, and Momolu undressed. They waded out into the water together with Flumbo's hand resting on Momolu's shoulder. The touch felt good, and when Momolu knew his father was gaining support for his stiff leg, he was happy. The right hand was no longer working against the left.

They swam up and down close to the shore, and then they came out and rested on the sand. The sun was hot. The water soon dried and left a thin layer of white salt over their dark skins.

While they were both at rest, they talked, about the brightness of the sun and the blueness of the clear sea water. It was so different from the brown water of the river at Lojay. At first their talk was of little things. Nothing they said was important, and nothing was really funny, but they laughed together and they were happy.

They were quiet for a while; then Flumbo spoke. "When my son is as old as his father is now," he said, "he will be wiser, but he will still do foolish things, and his old heart will still have foolish thoughts."

Flumbo got up and started running toward the water. Momolu followed, seeing his father limp as he waded out up to his waist before his body shot forward into the spray. They swam overhand straight out from the shore, Flumbo in front, Momolu close behind him.

It would be deep, but neither felt in danger. The smooth surface of the water rolled in long gentle swells. It was easier to swim in the sea than in the river at home. It was good.

Suddenly Flumbo turned. He waved Momolu

back. "Guns!" he shouted. "Soldiers shoot at us."

Momolu lifted his head and shook the water from his ears. For true, he heard guns firing on the shore and he thought he heard the whine of bullets overhead. He could not be sure because he was not used to the sound. He turned with Flumbo, and they swam back, matching stroke for stroke. Flumbo could have forged ahead, but he stayed with his son.

Each time Momolu slowed to shake the water from his ears, he heard the firing and the whining of bullets in the air. No soldiers were in sight. Momolu and Flumbo could not be sure whether those who fired were up on the hill or down by the beach. It could be that they thought their prisoners were trying to escape, but now they could surely see that Flumbo and Momolu were returning to give themselves up.

As they neared the beach, Flumbo called out, "Wait! Keep low. I go first. Wait!"

As Momolu crouched in the water, the sound of firing and the whistling song of bullets was very close. The shouts of those who fired came to him. Ahead he could see Flumbo clearly as he walked up the beach, his hands raised high over his head.

A whistle blew. Loud orders were called. The shooting stopped.

Flumbo stood motionless, while over the low rise beyond the beach, soldiers ran toward him.

Momolu got his feet under him and came out of the water, holding his own hands high. Soldiers shoved and pulled them both and had them stand before an angry sergeant, who shouted words at them in his own language which Momolu and Flumbo could not understand. But no one pointed a gun at either of them, and some of the soldiers were laughing. After telling them by signs to lower their hands, the sergeant turned and walked away, his men hurrying after him.

It was at Poobak's house that they finally learned what had happened.

"No, my good brothers," Poobak said, "no man shot to harm you. The soldiers were shooting in what we call target practice. Soldiers must learn to shoot. They did not know you were in the water."

"For true," Flumbo agreed. "When we heard the guns, we could not see the men who held them, and for true, they could not see us."

Flumbo and Poobak talked together of guns and hunting. Flumbo did not own a gun himself, but he had often shot with one belonging to Chief Logomo. The men of Lojay said he was a good hunter. The gun he used had two barrels, and with each shot many bullets fired. The army gun, Poobak explained, had only one barrel, and with each shot only one bullet fired, but it was a powerful gun and would go straight and far to reach its mark.

"Tomorrow," he said, "I myself go for target practice. I will ask my sergeant to let you go with me and shoot."

"Will they let me go with you and shoot?" asked Momolu.

Poobak and Flumbo looked at Momolu. Neither spoke for some time; then Poobak answered. "Guns are for men. Is my little brother yet a man?"

Momolu knew that he was only fourteen years old. He had been told that he was born during the first storm of the rainy season. When the rainy season came again, he would be fifteen. Then, according to the custom of the Kewpessie people, he would be old enough to claim the rights of a young man. Perhaps before they left the barracks, the first rains would fall. If so, he would be able to say that he was a man, and he would learn to shoot.

Anyway, he told himself, he could go and watch the others. He would hear the thing explained, and when his chance came, he would already understand.

16

The next afternoon when the soldiers carrying guns marched from the barracks square, Poobak followed with Momolu and Flumbo. At the place for target practice the soldiers spread out in a long thin line. Closer to the water, at a distance which Poobak said was a hundred yards, Momolu could see the targets standing in a row. Poobak's sergeant told Poobak to take his Kewpessie friends to one end of the line, and he pointed to the target at which they were to shoot.

Poobak showed Flumbo and Momolu his gun and explained how it worked, calling each part by name. He showed them how it was aimed, how the round ball in the middle of the target should line up on the sights. Momolu would not be permitted

176

to shoot, but while the heavy gun was still un-
loaded, Poobak let him hold it and aim and
squeeze the trigger.

Shots began to ring out all along the line. At
first the sound of each shot was frightening, but it
was not long before Momolu found that he liked
the noise. The smell of burnt gunpowder in his
nose was good. He only wished that he too might
shoot.

"Now I will tell you the three rules for a gun,"
Poobak said. "You must remember them and always follow them, and Momolu, when you are a
man, you must not forget.

"First"—he held up a finger—"always respect
a gun; respect it as you would a wise old man, and
never play with it.

"Second"—he held up two fingers—"know
the gun you use; know it inside and outside and
understand its parts; then you, and not the gun,
will be the master.

"Third"—he held up three fingers—"and this
is the greatest of the three, never point a gun at a
man unless you are ready to kill him, for killing is
all a gun is good for."

Poobak fired first, and then Flumbo took his

turn. They fired in different positions, standing and kneeling and lying flat on the ground, and every position that Poobak and his father took to shoot, Momolu without a gun also took.

The sergeant was going up and down behind the line, correcting mistakes and answering the questions of his men, scolding those that fired badly and sometimes taking the gun in his own hands to show them how to use it.

After he watched Flumbo shoot, he spoke to Poobak, looking pleased. "Sergeant says," Poobak interpreted, "that your eye is good and your finger is quick, although you do not hold the gun as you should."

Standing behind Flumbo where he knelt, the sergeant moved Flumbo's right arm higher and brought his left elbow a little lower under the gun.

Momolu was watching. He moved his arms into the same position. "Do I hold my gun as I should?" he asked Poobak.

Momolu was still not holding a gun; he was only going through the motions. The sergeant laughed and told Poobak to let the boy shoot.

Momolu peered down the sights. He pressed his

cheek hard against the wood and held the stock as tight as he could against his shoulder. When the black ball of the target was set just right between the sights, he pulled the trigger.

The gun spoke. It kicked into his shoulder with painful force. It hurt and stung his cheek. For a moment the sound deafened him, but the sergeant and Poobak and even Flumbo were well pleased, for on the target a new hole showed in the round black ball.

"Bull's-eye!" the sergeant said.

"Bull's-eye!" Poobak repeated. "His first shot is a bull's-eye! This Momolu shoots like an old soldier the very first time!"

Momolu shot many times after that. He did not again score a bull's-eye, but his shooting was good.

As they walked back up the hill behind the soldiers, Flumbo said, "The guns the soldiers use are better than any in Lojay. Some day we ourselves will own one. We will hunt and bring home plenty of fresh meat for our pots. Flumbo and his son will hunt together."

"For true," Momolu agreed, "Flumbo and his son will kill fresh meat for all the pots of Lojay."

180

17

Poobak was the one who gave Flumbo and Momolu their orders, and Flumbo watched closely to see that Momolu did his part well. Every morning they first swept the floors of all the barracks. When they finished the floors, they swept with palm branches the hard-packed paths around the parade ground and between the buildings.

Poobak did not stand guard over them. Captain Johnson, whose prisoners they were, seldom saw them, although Poobak said that he spoke of them often and asked how they were getting along. There were other prisoners at the barracks, and they worked all day under guards who carried clubs and whips and used them freely.

Each day after Momolu and Flumbo were

through with their yard work, they kept busy at tasks they found for themselves. Flumbo netted fish in the fashion of the Kewpessie people and took the fish he caught to Poobak's wife. Those she could not use she gave to her friends, who smiled at Flumbo and gave him their thanks.

While Flumbo fished, Momolu helped in what the soldiers called the shop. He cleaned floors and carried things and often stood and watched while the men did things with machines and tools which Momolu knew were useful but could not understand.

Each Sunday Jalla-Malla walked out to the barracks to visit his friends. The first time he came, he brought food and clean clothes, but Poobak helped Flumbo and Momolu to explain that there was no need for anything. Jalla-Malla reported that Tinsoo and Nisa-Way had returned to Lojay, and that Flumbo's canoe was being cared for by trusted friends. Jalla-Malla could see for himself that the food at Poobak's house was good and that there was plenty of it. Momolu himself washed their clothes and smoothed them with hot irons.

Flumbo was not altogether unhappy. He began to be interested in the activities of the soldiers, as

Momolu was, asking questions of Poobak and sharing his new thoughts with his son. Sometimes he would use the American tongue to say "Good morning" and "Good-bye" and "I go now," and they laughed together at the mistakes they made when they tried to say hard words like "headquarters" and "ammunition." Together they watched and admired whatever they saw about the barracks, as a visitor is supposed to, not staring and laughing or showing dislike. Flumbo, as well as Momolu, looked as though he were pleased, and Momolu heard him say, "Thank you," to a soldier who showed kindness.

In the late afternoon, after the time of about one moon had passed at the barracks, father and son stood together watching the ceremony of the flag. On both sides of the square, soldiers stood in double lines, with six soldiers in a short line in front. The music of the bugle was sounding, and the flag with its one white star was being lowered while every man stood very straight, his right hand held to his forehead in salute. Flumbo and Momolu stood very straight too. Momolu would have saluted the flag of the government of Liberia, but he knew Flumbo would not like him to do so.

Just the same, as he watched the cloth of red and white and blue, he was thinking that although he was part of the Kewpessie people, he was glad he was part of the Liberian nation as well. Poobak had said "All Kewpessies are Liberians, but all Liberians are not Kewpessies."

After the flag was down, the soldiers were ordered to lower their hands, and then they were dismissed. They turned away to go to their evening meal, and the officers went back to headquarters.

Walking behind his father, Momolu started down the hill toward Poobak's house where he knew a good meal of fish and rice was waiting. They were nearly there when Poobak came running up from behind, to call them back.

"Captain Johnson says you must come quick-quick," he said. "He makes big palaver."

When they reached the level parade ground at the top of the hill, Momolu walked beside his father, marching, and Flumbo held himself straight so he would not limp.

Their captain was standing outside the door of headquarters, talking with other officers.

"Flumbo! Momolu!" he called out, smiling.

"Good morning," Flumbo said.

"Thank you," was Momolu's greeting.

The other officers laughed as the captain bowed and said something to Poobak.

Poobak said, "Now Captain Johnson wants to know what you will say."

"Tell the captain for me that all his soldier people are good to Flumbo and Momolu, his son," Flumbo said.

Then the captain asked through Poobak, "Does Flumbo still hate soldiers?"

For a moment Flumbo's eyes fell; then he said, speaking loudly and looking over the captain's head, "These men do not make war just now. I know some of them, and in this place they treat me as a friend, but they are soldiers, and soldiers are the enemies of country people. A man must hate the enemies of his people."

Poobak talked a long time with the captain and the other officers also. Finally he turned back to Flumbo again.

"Captain Johnson says now his heart cannot lie down," he said. "He wants to see you a full free man, but you yourself say soldiers are your enemy. Tomorrow the captain starts a new trip to the bush. The way will lead through Kewpessie country. Soldiers will go with him and he will need people to carry his hammock and supplies. He says that you and your son can go with them to help with the carrying if you agree to keep the laws of government."

Flumbo's head bowed in deep thought. Then speaking slowly he said to Poobak, "Ask the captain if the soldiers go in peace or if they go to kill."

When Poobak asked the question, the officers laughed, and Captain Johnson gave Poobak the answer.

"The captain says that this trip is for road palaver. It is not for killing, but a soldier must go where he is told, and he must do what he has to do. No man can say what tomorrow will bring."

Flumbo looked hard at the face of the captain. Momolu was afraid his father would not agree. Then Flumbo spoke loudly using American words, "I go now!"

18

~~~~~~

It seemed to Momolu that he had hardly gone to sleep before his father was shaking him and calling his name. He sat up and rubbed his eyes. Soldiers were moving half-dressed through the barracks, and outside excited voices were calling. A light, like that from a great fire, shone through the windows. Flumbo said that they must hurry; there was no time to go and wash. Momolu reached for his pants and shirts where he had left them hanging on a peg. They were not there.

"Clean clothes," Flumbo said, pointing to a folded pile on the floor. There were two pairs of soldier pants and two shirts, clean and freshly ironed. Flumbo was wearing his robe, but he was making for himself a bundle of his blanket and of other khaki-colored garments.

A soldier came for them. Outside at the open end of the square stood two trucks, with their headlights blazing brighter than any fire of gumwood. A sergeant's whistle sounded, the soldier started running, and Flumbo and Momolu ran behind him.

"Flumbo, Momolu! This way!" Poobak called and led his Kewpessie brothers to the first truck. They climbed up, and the soldiers already inside made room for the newcomers on the benchlike seats along the sides. Down the middle were piled boxes and bags. There was no roof overhead.

"For one day we will ride," Poobak said. "Tonight we will camp at the end of the road; the next days we will walk."

The soldiers who were not going and the wives and children of those who were crowded around the loaded trucks. Over and over Momolu heard the American words, "Good-bye" and "God bless."

A strap was fastened across the back, and after the sergeant had made a final count, Captain Johnson and two of his brother officers came out from headquarters. They looked into both trucks and satisfied themselves that all was well. Then the captain climbed into the front to sit with the driver, and the sergeant blew his whistle again as he took his place with the driver of the second truck.

There was a roar as the truck's motor came alive. Momolu did not know whether Flumbo had ever before ridden in a truck. In the bright light from the second truck, he could see Flumbo's face clearly. He sat very straight, his eyes shut tight. Momolu laid his hand on his father's knee. It was trembling from more than the movement of the truck.

"Never mind, Pa." Momolu leaned toward his father to speak. "I rode before. The driver is the master of the truck. I have seen it."

With a jerk the truck moved forward. From those inside the truck and from those left behind, a cheer went up. Momolu himself was startled by the sudden motion and noise, but soon the truck was moving smoothly down the hill. Turning from the side road into the broad clean highway, it rolled along, climbing the first long hill faster than a man, faster than a horse, could run.

Ahead Momolu saw how the lights made the roadway bright as day. Behind them the form of the other truck could not be seen. Only its two lights, shining like the eyes of a great beast, came steadily toward them, lighting the road and the forest through which it ran.

Some of the soldiers talked among themselves. Others—and Poobak was one of them—drew their blankets over their heads and slept.

The sun came up ahead of them, and Momolu knew they were traveling east. They rolled by a cluster of houses, where people waved and called greetings. Momolu leaned far out of the truck to answer, but Flumbo neither waved nor called out.

"Prisoners!" he said bitterly. "We are prisoners. We go back to our own countryside as prisoners."

Momolu said nothing. Poobak had not heard.

Flumbo went on, "I want to go back to my own people, but I will never walk into Lojay as a prisoner of soldiers. I will run away—or I will die. I will never be a prisoner in Lojay!"

Momolu knew that it would do no good to say that they were not like other prisoners or that his father could have made peace with the men of government. He looked forward to being in Kewpessie country. To hear the speech and the music of his people, to eat with them and to see them dancing—these would give him joy. He hoped now that the way would not lead through Lojay, but this was only for the sake of his father.

It was still early morning when they came down a long hill toward a wide river. They had already crossed a number of streams, some of them by bridges. At others the driver had cut the speed and eased the truck down the bank to roll through shallow water. Now the river ahead was surely too wide and deep for them to cross, and there was no bridge, for the road seemed to end.

The truck stopped before it reached the water. At the side of the road a Liberian flag floated over a small white house surrounded by country houses.

"Ferry station," Poobak said.

Soldiers and their families ran out to surround the two trucks. There was laughter and glad cries of delight. An officer came out of the house to greet Captain Johnson.

"Here we will eat," Poobak said. "Then we will cross the river."

Flumbo and Momolu were treated like guests. The sergeant sent Poobak with Flumbo and Momolu to the house of a soldier who had already cooked a large pot of rice and other foods. Flumbo objected saying that three extra bellies were too many for one man to fill.

When the soldier heard this from Poobak, he laughed. "Come and see," he said.

He led them beyond the houses and turned around so that they could see.

Stretched out for more space than was covered by all the town of Lojay were field after field of heavy green leaves, rising and stretching over the hills in wave after wave. The soldier showed them rows of cassava plants, a large bed of peppers, a field of corn, a field of sweet potatoes.

"This is a farm run by the ferry-station soldiers," Poobak explained. "The Liberian officer in charge has been to a special school in far America, where he learned the American way to make things grow. Here you see the small plants—the trees on that side, standing in straight rows like soldiers, are full of coconuts. On the other side, though you cannot see from here, are paw-paw trees. Down by the river, bananas grow—more bananas than there are grains in a bag of rice. And for meat—well, on the other side of the road, cows are feeding in green fields, and white chickens live in their own houses and lay eggs every day."

"But what can they do with so much food?" Flumbo asked.

"When the trucks leave us and return to the barracks tomorrow, each one will be filled," Poobak answered. "So it is that the soldiers at the barracks are able to eat well."

With so much food at hand, Flumbo was quite willing to eat. It was like a feast. When they left, Momolu's pockets were filled with peanuts, and in his hands he carried oranges and bananas.

As they climbed back into the truck, Momolu began to wonder again how they were to cross the river. Some of the soldiers were already at the waterside. The driver started his motor, and driving slowly, he eased the heavy machine down the hill. As they neared the water, they could see a large flatboat drawn close to the bank.

"That is the ferry," Poobak told them. "Now we go aboard."

When the truck was safely stationed in the center of the platform, two ferrymen poled the boat across the river, and as they worked they sang.

At the far bank the truck was driven ashore and up the hill where it waited for the ferrymen to pole the boat back to the opposite side and bring the second truck across.

At the ferry station, they had eaten well. Every soldier on the truck had brought more food, and that afternoon they did not have to stop to eat again.

Near the coast the road had been wide, so that trucks and cars coming and going could freely pass. In the afternoon the road was narrow and not so straight. They drove through heavy forests, where trees of cyprus and bomba and mahogany grew so close together that their branches met overhead, shutting out the sun. They drove up steep hills and down, and along the shore of a lake where rocks had been cut to form a bank for the roadway. They passed through fields of high elephant grass, where the tops of the grass bent under the wind like waves of the great sea now far behind them at the coast.

"Who makes the roads?" Momolu asked. "Are roads here like rivers, because the gods have made them so?"

"Not so," Poobak answered. "The government

sends soldiers to help build roads, and the people in the country do their part."

"But people in the country would not work to make the roads if government did not send soldiers who kill," Flumbo said.

"Soldiers do not kill to make a road," Poobak said. "It is twelve years that I have been a soldier. I have seen war, but I have never seen it fought because of a road. I have seen soldiers and country people working together. I myself cut trees and moved rock and carried dirt in baskets on my head to help make this road."

Momolu could understand why roads were important to soldiers. He knew that it would take many days to walk the distance they had driven in only part of a day.

"But why do the country people help?" he asked.

"Those who are wise help," Poobak answered. "Those who have traveled understand that roads bring a better life to all the people. Roads open up the country for trade. Country people can sell their palm oil and nuts and piassava, and they can buy the things they need. Where there are roads those of different towns and different speech can get to know each other—Kewpessies and Golas, Bassas and Mendes, Krus and Manos. Then they learn to live in peace.

"And more"—Poobak looked at Flumbo as he spoke—"where roads go through the country, people know their government is not against them."

"In our Kewpessie country, we have no roads." Flumbo said. "I like it better so."

"You will see." Poobak made a wide gesture with his arm. "You will see. Before the sun goes down, we will be in Kewpessie country, and you will see the people making their road. Next year Swahoo will be joined to Cape Roberts, and in time so will your own Lojay."

Momolu thought for a moment. "Then Lojay will not be the same," he said.

"No," said Poobak. "It will not be the same."

19

"Day comes now!" A cheerful voice awakened Momolu the next morning. "Day comes now! Get your feet under you. The road you walk today is long-O!"

Momolu rubbed the sleep from his eyes. The words had been spoken in Kewpessie, but the voice was not that of either Flumbo or Poobak. A man he did not know was looking down at him where he lay on the clay floor. Around him others were talking in the pleasant Kewpessie tongue.

He threw back his blanket and laughed as he remembered.

When the trucks had reached this place, they were in Kewpessie country. During the late afternoon they had not been able to move with much

198

speed because the road was still being built. Hundreds of men—Golas and Kewpessies—were working with picks and shovels and baskets and wheelbarrows. Machines, such as Momolu had never before seen, were moving dirt with scrapers and scoops. Hills were being cut away and low places filled.

Each working group had its own music. Drummers sang as they beat out their rhythm, and every man who worked moved to the beat. Crude camps of temporary palm-leaf shelters had been set up. It was at the last of these that the trucks stopped just before dark. Lightning flashed high in the sky, and the sound of thunder rumbled over the noise of the trucks.

"Soon," Poobak said, "the dry season will be finished. Then the country people will no longer work on the road. They will go back to their own houses and farms. During the rains only the soldiers will work on the road."

Momolu was tired when he got out of the truck. He found it odd that he should be tired, for all day long he had done no work. He had only sat with the others, while the truck carried the heavy load of men and supplies. He wanted to sit by the fire and listen to Kewpessie talk and hear Kewpessie drums and songs, but he was tired, and when they showed him where he should sleep, he wrapped his blanket around him and slept through the night without awakening.

"The road you walk today is long-O!"

For true, this place was not an army camp. In the barracks the bugle sounded and the sergeant's whistle signaled for time to get up and time to eat and time to assemble. Here there was neither bugle nor whistle. Here the drums beat out, and the drummers sang that now was the time to wash and to get the camp cleaned up. Before the job was done, the drums were saying that every man must eat—must eat strong food; heavy meat and sweet palm oil and plenty of pepper so that arms would be strong to lift the heavy load, so that legs would be like iron to work on the long road. Then the big bass drum sounded, and the workers gathered in the road around their leaders. They did not stand stiff and erect in straight lines like soldiers. They wore no uniforms and carried no guns. Most of them wore only loincloths, and carried only the tools with which they would work. Even among the soldiers who worked, the only part of their uniform that they wore was the round red cap on their heads.

"A soldier without his khaki and gun looks the same as any man," Momolu thought.

When those who were working on the road had gone off to their day's work, the sergeant for the first time blew his whistle. His twenty soldiers formed in line. With their guns on their shoulders, in their uniforms, they looked truly like the soldiers they were.

Turning toward Flumbo and Momolu, the captain beckoned. As Momolu and Flumbo hurried forward, the captain called Poobak from the line to translate for him.

"Captain says that now you are to do your part," Poobak interpreted. "We are to journey in Kewpessie country and the men who carry his hammock and supplies are Kewpessie. Flumbo will be headman for the carriers."

Flumbo raised his hand in question. "Ask the captain," he said to Poobak, "if the carriers are prisoners, for if the carriers are Kewpessie free men, they will not listen to the word of one who is a prisoner."

Poobak talked for Flumbo and then he gave the

captain's answer in the captain's own way. "They are free men, and Flumbo is headman. So be it! That palaver is finished."

The captain spoke again then, looking at Momolu, and Poobak translated for him, "Captain says Momo will have a special load."

When they were on their way, Momolu marched straighter than anyone else in the line.

The sergeant led the way with one soldier close behind him. Next came the heavy bass drum strapped on the back of a Kewpessie man. The soldier drummer swung his clublike sticks in wide arcs, sending the drum's great voice rolling across the hills and valleys.

The captain rode in his hammock, slung on the frame that rested on the heads of four men selected by Flumbo for their height and strength. Momolu walked close behind the hammock, and twenty soldiers followed, marching in single file. Then came the carriers with bundles and boxes on their heads. Flumbo was the last man in the line. It was his duty to see that the others kept moving and that no one dropped his load or jumped out of line and escaped into the bush. Flumbo carried nothing, but Momolu carried for the captain the things he valued most: his magic box called radio, his great gun which Poobak said was powerful enough to kill an elephant, and a leather case containing papers and books.

"Gun-bearer," the captain had said as Poobak and the sergeant adjusted the load. The gun was slung on Momolu's back. The radio hung at his side from straps which went over his shoulder. The heavy case of books was balanced on his head.

So they were coming back into Kewpessie country. Momolu felt something like pride because he had been trusted to be a gun-bearer, but he felt shame too because he had been the cause and the center of all the trouble that had come upon his proud father.

The load Momolu carried was heavy. It had not seemed so at first, but as the sun rose higher, the day became hot. His clothes were soon soaked with sweat. At their first stop for rest Flumbo helped him to make a pad of his shirt so that the heavy radio would no longer bruise his side. Flumbo had little to say.

The way led along a well-beaten trail. Some day

it would be a wide road for autos to travel. Some of the carriers knew the country well. In every town friends came out to greet them.

When they stopped at a town for the night, the chief and all the people made them welcome. They were used to soldiers and treated them as friends. Momolu found himself to be the center of attraction wherever he spent the night. He forgot his own problems. It was his first chance to talk with boys of his own age about the wonders his eyes had seen at Cape Roberts. Great ships, autos, planes, houses, the mission, and the reading of books—all these he described in answer to their questions. Momolu spoke with great pride.

20

~~~~~~

In the morning he could hardly get his eyes open when Poobak wakened him. "Day comes now," Poobak said, "and there is trouble!"

It was Flumbo's leg. Flumbo was not accustomed to so much walking, and now he was unable to stand. His weak leg was swollen. The skin felt hot when Momolu tried to help his father by rubbing it with oil and pepper.

"You must tell the captain," Flumbo said, "that he must leave me. I cannot run away. If I die he will lose his prisoner, but if I grow strong again, I will wait here for him. These are my people. They will help me. Momolu must go on. He must act for me. If I die, Momolu will repay Jalla-Malla the five bags of rice."

The captain came to see Flumbo. He talked with Poobak in the American tongue; then beckoning for Momolu to follow him, he went back to the guesthouse where he had spent the night. Momolu watched while he took from the leather case a large book which he turned back and forth and then read with a deep frown.

Then he had Momolu shift the boxes of supplies to find a white box with a large red cross stamped on it. The captain unlocked the box, and when he lifted the lid, Momolu saw many small packages, and in the lid itself bright knives and scissors and other instruments that Momolu did not know. When the captain had selected from it what he wanted, he started back to the house where they had left Flumbo.

Drums were beating. A crowd had gathered near the palaver house. Carriers and people of the village stood in a large circle where a medicine man was dancing. The circle opened to let the captain through. Flumbo lay on a mat in the center of the circle. He was watching the dancer who swirled about in a skirt of black monkey fur.

The medicine man did not wear a mask, but his face was painted with white and red in such a way that his real nose and mouth and eyes could hardly be seen. He waved a switch of horsehair. His assistant threw powder into the air. His voice was not loud, but at one time Momolu heard the words:

> Be you from water or be you from land,
> I tell you now to leave this man.

Momolu stopped and watched, saying nothing. The beating of the drums grew louder and faster. The dancer whirled faster and leaped higher. Then suddenly he turned and ran away.

Now the captain moved forward, and resting on one knee, he spread a clean white paper on the mat. On this he laid some things as he told Poobak what to say.

"Captain Johnson says he comes to help the Kewpessie medicine man," Poobak told the people. "He says Flumbo must eat a small, small thing, and then captain will put more medicine in Flumbo's leg. For this he uses what he calls needle."

Flumbo did not move while the captain stuck the needle in the thick part of his leg.

The captain spoke again as he got to his feet, and Poobak told Flumbo what he said. "Captain

Johnson says he cannot leave you in a strange house."

"So!" Flumbo spoke with anger. "The captain fears to lose a prisoner."

Poobak did not put Flumbo's words into American speech, but the captain seemed to understand. He laughed and shook his head. "I be captain," he said.

When they moved again, Flumbo was riding in the hammock, and he was asleep. The captain was walking in front with the sergeant.

He led his men from the wide trail into a narrow path, which was overgrown in places by high bush and tangled vines. Sometimes their march was very slow. The morning sun was on their left, so Momolu knew they were moving southward. Later they crossed a wide valley of high grass, and beyond the valley, they entered a forest. There was no clear trail, but the great trees cast a heavy shade and there was little undergrowth of bush. At a stream they stopped to eat and rest. Momolu went to his father. The hammock carriers had laid him, still sleeping, on the ground. Pooback came when he noticed Momolu trying to arouse Flumbo.

"Never mind, Momo," Poobak said. "It is the captain's strong medicine that holds him."

"What does he want, that captain?" Momolu asked. "We are already his prisoners. Will he kill my father and then me?"

"Your talk is foolish, boy." Poobak was very serious. "See—he has turned off from the main trail to find the shortest way to Lojay."

Momolu felt his heart turn over. "But this will pile shame on my father's head," he said. "The captain is bringing him to his house as a prisoner. All the people will see him so."

"Not so," Poobak shook his head. "It is only Flumbo himself who makes Flumbo a prisoner. If Flumbo were really a prisoner, would the captain have his people walk two days through deep bush to take him home? I have tried to make your father understand, but his heart is full of hate for government and soldiers. I am his Kewpessie brother, but he thinks I am his enemy. It is you who must make him understand."

Poobak said many more things of the same kind, and although Momolu would not criticize his father or take a stand against him, he knew that Poobak was right.

The drummers were sounding the call to march. Soldiers were falling in line. The Kewpessie man who had taken Flumbo's place was shouting his orders. Poobak went back to his place, and as Momolu watched the four hammock men straighten under their load, he tried to know what his father would want him to say.

21

~~~~~~

In the middle of the afternoon they came to Swahoo, the largest town in the Kewpessie section and the home of the paramount chief. It was less than a day's journey from Swahoo to Lojay.

Around the market square, white traders and African merchants had large shops. The people were used to seeing soldiers. They hardly turned to look as the soldiers and carriers, marching two by two instead of single file, marched through the town to camp in the barracks on the far hill. No roads joined Swahoo with the outside world, but radio towers rose above the barracks, and a small plane waited in its house beside a landing strip.

Flumbo was awake when the company stopped. He told Momolu that his leg did not hurt, but when he tried to stand, he fell to the ground. Captain Johnson gave him more medicine, and then Flumbo rested quietly on the mat where the carriers laid him.

It was good to be in the shelter of the barracks that night, for the first rain of the season fell. Now Momolu knew that he was fifteen years old, old enough to go to the tribal training camp. In special places in the deep bush, boys were taught the secret things of manhood. Priests of the bush and medicine men and bush devils taught the hidden meanings of life and death, the deep truths that lie between a man and his woman, and many mysteries of gods and of devils.

After a storm with thunder and lightning and high wind, the rain fell steadily, and those inside the barracks settled down to sleep. Momolu lay awake on his mat, while all about him men were breathing deep and snoring. He knew he would have to make his father understand the things that Poobak had said, and there was more. Flumbo would have to know that the eyes of his son were looking toward a new way, a way that would not lead Momolu into the dark forest to learn the things of country life. It would lead him rather to a school with books where all the things that man has learned are set down for all to see. Like John, son of Jalla-Malla, like Birmah, now called David, like the writing soldier at the commissioner's, Momolu too would know how to read.

The next morning Flumbo seemed wide awake and fresh. When they told him they were in Swahoo, he knew they were near home. He said that his leg was as good as ever, but the captain sent Poobak to say that he should remain in the hammock. Momolu could see that his father was worried. Flumbo knew, although he had not been told, that they were going to Lojay.

In the late morning they stopped in a shady place on the bank of a small river. Momolu found Flumbo resting himself by walking about, while the others were lying down or washing themselves in the river.

"It is not my leg," Flumbo said. "It is my head and my heart." Momolu said nothing, and Flumbo went on, "In my head I know that all soldiers are enemies to country people, but in my heart I feel that these soldiers are my brothers."

"For true," Momolu agreed.

"Now Poobak is a Kewpessie man. For me and for my son, he does everything he can. Is he not my brother? But Poobak is a brother to the sergeant and the others and all of them are like sons of the captain, and how can I hate the captain?"

Now it was Momolu's turn to talk, and the words came from him quickly. It was not as though he were a small boy speaking to his father. He talked as he thought, and Flumbo listened. Then Flumbo spoke again, and they were still talking together when the whistle blew and Momolu hurried off to get his load.

It was time to move on. The captain came with Poobak to translate for him. "The captain says that if your leg is strong again he will take the hammock because his own legs are tired," Poobak told Flumbo.

Flumbo slapped his thigh; he kicked and jumped to show that he was fit to walk.

The captain nodded his head and said something which Poobak put into Kewpessie speech. "The captain wants to know if Flumbo would still lead the men of Lojay against the soldiers."

Flumbo did not speak for a while. He seemed to

be searching in his heart for the right words. He looked over at Momolu, and then he spoke to the captain.

"I will speak the truth as my father has taught me to speak. I would not make a fight against the soldiers again, and now I know that the soldiers are not the enemies of the country people. These soldiers are my brothers."

After Captain Johnson heard Flumbo's answer, he gave Poobak another question to ask. "By and by when the government comes to Lojay to make the road, will the men of Lojay help?"

"They will help," Flumbo answered as soon as he heard the question. "They will help, and Flumbo, if he is in Lojay, will be their headman. You will see."

The captain smiled when Poobak told him Flumbo's words; and Poobak too was smiling when he spoke again for the captain. "The captain says Flumbo will soon be in Lojay. Now Flumbo is a free Kewpessie man. The palaver is finished."

And so they came to Lojay.

The people of the town had heard the drum, and they seemed to know that Flumbo and his son were coming home. They came out to meet them on the trail, waving palm branches. They made music with their drums and gourds and with horns and pipes and whistles. One of Bama's drummers danced on bamboo stilts, and with each step bells jangled on the bamboo poles that served as legs.

After their first greeting, Portee, Flumbo's wife, and Sindah, his daughter, and all of Sindah's children and many other people who loved him clung to him and made him the center of their own party.

Slung with gun and radio and weighted with the bag of books on his head, Momolu tried hard not to look proud. Dairku and Billidee and all his other friends, each wanted to carry something for him, but he had to tell them that the captain would not like it. Then his friends came and joined the line of march with him, and each one walked as though he too had something special to carry.

By the time they reached the center of the town, they were no longer marching; they were dancing. Feet were moving together; hands were clapping; a song had started, and different ones made lines to sing a verse with everyone joining in the chorus:

Flumbo and his son come home.
Flumbo and his son come home.
Flumbo and his son come home,
We will make them happy.

Soon there was feasting, and Flumbo sat at his
own house with Poobak and the sergeant and the
other soldiers while Portee and her friends whom
she called sisters brought food to them. The sun
was still high, and while the people were eating,
the sound of laughter and music was everywhere.

When everyone was filled, the town became
quiet. Men slept in the palaver house and in the
narrow strips of shade under the overhanging
roofs. Women slept inside their houses. Children
slept anywhere. Only chickens and goats stayed
awake, and they found plenty of scraps for their
own feast.

The whole town slept while it was hot; then all
the people rose. They went first to wash themselves and then to dress in their finest clothes.
Just before dark they gathered at the palaver
house. A wide brass basin of gumwood blazed in
front of the platform where Chief Logomo's great
chair waited.

Once again Momolu was seated inside with the
men. His friends and all the women were outside

the palaver house, but they too could see and hear over the waist-high wall. And for the first time the soldiers were not all gathered together in one place. They were seated inside with the Kewpessie men as if they were the brothers of those whose food they had eaten.

Bama took up his heavy sticks and struck the great bass drum. The people stopped talking while Bama beat out the call of honor, and then everyone bowed low and said his words of honor: "Our strong protector, our father, Logomo."

When the rhythm of the drum changed, Momolu raised his head. Chief Logomo had taken his place with Captain Johnson beside him on his right. Bomo-Koko stood directly behind the chief, only his head showing above Chief Logomo's chair. The old men of the council were filing in with Tinsoo at their head. Each old man was followed by a small boy carrying a low stool.

When stools had been placed around the chief, each council member gathered the skirts of his robe and lowered himself to sit straight, unsmiling, wise, attentive. Each sat except old Tinsoo who was to speak for Chief Logomo.

In his high-pitched voice Tinsoo said that the

chief wanted to know if any would care to go back to the other palaver when the captain and his soldiers first came to Lojay. All the people exclaimed no, and if anyone thought the idea funny, no one laughed or said so.

Then Tinsoo said that the chief did not want to waste their time by telling them how the mighty captain of the government had protected their brother Flumbo and his son Momolu. When he paused and looked about all the people said with one voice, "Tell us Tinsoo. Tell us."

Old Tinsoo looked as if he were surprised. He turned around and leaned over to speak to the chief. While the drummers beat out the rhythm, the people said over and over, "Tell us, Tinsoo. Tell us." They clapped their hands and stamped their feet on the hard-packed clay, saying over and over, "Tell us, Tinsoo. Tell us."

So Tinsoo told them, but it was not the story as Momolu knew it. Tinsoo was a good storyteller, and Momolu had always believed his other stories. Now he spoke of the captain as if he were a kindly chief and magician who had stricken chains from the hands of Flumbo and his son when evil men would have kept them bound. The captain had taken them to his house, Tinsoo said, and provided them with rice and tender meat and crisp fried fish and soft green vegetables and sweet fruits and melons. He had taught them how to shoot the finest guns and brought them for the space of a day in one of the government's mighty trucks. Then when Flumbo's leg was weak and painful, burning as though it were on fire, the captain had worked the magic of his medicine and made it well, so Flumbo came home as all could see, just the same.

Then Tinsoo talked about Momolu, the son of Flumbo. He had nothing bad to say; he did not speak of the upset canoe and the lost rice. He spoke only of how, like a worthy son, Momolu had risked the dangers of the journey with his father, as a companion more than as a son, and how, to pay the debt of his father, Momolu had offered his own young body in service.

While Tinsoo spoke, Bama was shaping a song, echoing Tinsoo's words and making them rhyme.

As Tinsoo finished his talk, he said, "Those words that you hear are the words of Logomo, chief of Lojay, through the mouth of his servant, Tinsoo."

Then Bama sang aloud, and with the chorus all joined in:

> Flumbo and his son come home.
> And we will make them happy.

While he sang the verses, Bama beat his drum softly, and all the people strained to listen to the words, their heads bobbing with the rhythm, their bodies swaying from side to side. At the chorus, Bama smashed down with both sticks as though he would break through the drumhead. The people shouted out the words and clapped their hands and looked on Momolu with admiration.

When the song ended, fresh wood was put on the fire in front of the platform. The dancing flames rose high, and light flooded the faces of those nearby. Four men lifted the great chair in which Chief Logomo sat and moved it forward to the edge of the platform.

The chief raised his hand. All the people watched him and waited to hear his word. He turned and looked about him to see if all his men of council were there. Then he looked out over the crowd and bent forward to peer into the darkness beyond the palaver house. At last he turned toward Momolu where he sat between Flumbo and Nisa-Way, and he smiled as he spoke.

"Our Momolu was a small boy only yesterday," he said. "A few days ago he was a baby sucking at his mother's breast. We have seen him growing up in his father's house and now we have seen him go forth into the world at his father's side and speaking out with the strong heart of a man.

"How can we understand the wonder of a baby coming from his mother's body or the strength of the young or the wisdom of the old?" he asked.

The people bowed their heads and murmured at the wisdom of their chief.

"Now new wonders are in the land," Logomo said. "From far America and other lands, white men bring new magic, greater than any we have seen before. And who can understand them? Can old Tinsoo? Can Flumbo? Can our Momolu?"

Momolu had never dared to speak in the palaver house. He had never been in the place of honor. Now his name had been called, and Chief Logomo had asked a question. He wanted to answer.

His own eyes had seen many wonders. He had

learned that trucks and airplanes and radios did not work by magic but by the direction of man. He had been told that men have put in books all the things they know and that those who read can learn whatever others know.

He started to move. As his legs straightened under him, Flumbo's hand reached out and held his robe. It was all like a dream. He pulled the cloth from Flumbo's hand and started walking forward.

The noise of the drum was stilled. Bama held his sticks motionless in the air. In the sudden silence Chief Logomo opened his eyes wide. "My son," the chief asked, "is there something in your heart that you would say?"

"If the chief of Lojay would hear Momolu?" He bowed low. It seemed he had nothing to fear, for it still seemed like a dream.

Chief Logomo was surprised, but he smiled his approval as he said, "Speak, my son."

"I, Momolu, have seen the things that we call magic," he said. "Now I do not understand so much, but I do know that some men understand, and someday I, Momolu, will understand."

226

ABOUT THE AUTHOR

Lorenz Graham was born in New Orleans, the son of a Methodist minister. In his junior year at the University of California at Los Angeles, he gave up his studies to teach in a Liberian mission. He became interested in the tribal culture of his students and decided that he should write about the African people.

When Mr. Graham returned to this country he was graduated from Virginia Union University. Since that time he has worked with young people as teacher and social worker. He is now a probation officer in Los Angeles.

Mr. Graham and his wife met in Liberia, where she too was a missionary. Together they revisited Africa before the writing of *I, Momolu* was finished.

ABOUT THE ILLUSTRATOR

John Biggers is head of the art department at Texas Southern University. During 1965–66 he served as visiting professor of art at the University of Wisconsin.

Dr. Biggers was born in Gastonia, North Carolina, and educated at Pennsylvania State University. In 1957, as a UNESCO fellow, he made an artist's study of life in West Africa.

Dr. Biggers' many honors include purchase awards from museums in Houston and Dallas; the Dallas Museum Award in Best Book Design for *Ananse: The Web of Life in Africa;* and the Architectural League's Honorable Mention in Mural Decoration. His work has been shown in museums and galleries in New York, Texas, and Pennsylvania.